Mr. Trunnell, Mat

Ship "Pirate"

T. Jenkins Hains

Alpha Editions

This edition published in 2023

ISBN : 9789357951517

Design and Setting By
Alpha Editions
www.alphaedis.com
Email - info@alphaedis.com

Contents

I

By some means, needless to record here, I found myself, not so many years ago, "on the beach" at Melbourne, in Australia.

To be on the beach is not an uncommon occurrence for a sailor in any part of the world; but, since the question is suggested, I will say that I was not a very dissipated young fellow of twenty-five, for up to that time I had never even tasted rum in any form, although I had followed the sea for seven years.

I had held a mate's berth, and as I did not care to ship before the mast on the first vessel bound out, I had remained ashore until a threatening landlord made it necessary for me to become less particular as to occupation.

It was a time when mates were plenty and men were few, so I made the rounds of the shipping houses with little hope of getting a chance to show my papers. These, together with an old quadrant, a nautical almanac, a thick pea coat, and a pipe, were all I possessed of this world's goods, and I carried the quadrant with me in case I should not succeed in signing on. I could "spout it," if need be, at some broker's, and thus raise a few dollars.

As I made my way along the water front, I noticed a fine clipper ship of nearly two thousand tons lying at a wharf. She was in the hands of a few riggers, who were sending aloft her canvas, which, being of a snowy whiteness, proclaimed her nationality even before I could see her hull. On reaching the wharf where she lay, I stopped and noticed that she was loaded deep, for her long black sides were under to within four feet of her main deck in the waist.

Her high bulwarks shut off my view of her deck; but, from the sounds that came down from there, I could tell that she was getting in the last of her cargo.

I walked to her stern and read her name in gilt letters: "Pirate, of Philadelphia." Then I remembered her. She was a Yankee ship of evil reputation, and although I wanted to get back to my home in New York, I turned away thankful that I was not homeward bound in that craft. She had come into port a month before and had reported three men missing from her papers. There were no witnesses; but the sight of the rest of the crew told the story of the disappearance of their shipmates, and the skipper had been clapped into jail. I had heard of the ruffian's sinister record before, and inwardly hoped he would get his deserts for his brutality, although I knew there was little chance for it. He belonged to the class of captains that was giving American packets the hard name they were getting, so I heartily wished him evil.

As I turned, looking up at the beautiful fabric with her long, tapering, t'gallant masts, topped with skysail yards fore and aft, and her tremendous lower yards nearly ninety feet across, I thought what a splendid ship she was. It made me angry to think of what a place she must be for the poor devils who would unwittingly ship aboard her. Only a sailor knows how much of suffering in blows and curses it cost to accomplish all that clean paint and scraped spar.

"Kind o' good hooker, hey?" said a voice close aboard me, and looking quickly aft I saw a man leaning over the taffrail. He was a strange-looking fellow, with a great hairy face and bushy head set upon the broadest of shoulders. As for his legs, he appeared not to have any at all, for the rail was but three feet high and his shoulders just reached above it; his enormously long arms were spread along the rail, elbows outward, and his huge hands folded over the bowl of a pipe which he sucked complacently.

"Not so bad to look at," I answered, meaningly.

"She *is* a brute in a seaway, but she keeps dry at both ends," assented the fellow, utterly ignoring my meaning. "It's always so with every hooker if she's deep. Some takes it forrad and aft, and some takes it amidships. It's all one s'long as she keeps a dry bilge. Come aboard."

I hesitated, and then climbed up the mizzen channels, which were level with the wharf.

"Short handed?" I suggested, reaching the deck.

"Naw, there's nobody but me an' the doctor in the after guard; we'll get a crew aboard early in the morning, though; skipper, too, if what they say is kerrect."

"Where's the captain?" I asked.

He looked queerly at me for a moment; then he spread his short legs wide apart, and thrust his great hands into his trousers pockets before speaking.

"Ain't ye never heard? Limbo, man, and a bad job, too." Here he made a motion with his hand around his neck which I understood.

"Murder?"

He nodded.

I hesitated about staying any longer, and he spoke up.

"Got a hog-yoke, I see," he said, "Be ye a mate?"

I told him I had been.

"Well, sink me, my boy, that's just what I am aboard here, and they'll be looking for another to match me. I saw what ye were when I first raised ye coming along the dock, and sez I, ye're just my size, my bully."

As he could have walked under my arm when extended horizontally, I saw he had no poor opinion of himself. However, his words conveyed a ray of hope.

"Is the mate with the skipper?" I asked.

"The second mate is, yep; but he won't raise bail. The old man might though, *quien sabe*? The agents will hail us to-night and settle matters, for we're on the load line and nigh steved. We can't wait."

I reflected a moment. Here was a possible chance for a mate's berth, and perhaps the skipper would not get bail, after all. In that case I thought I could hardly manage better, for my fear of the little mate was not overpowering. I was not exactly of a timid nature,—a man seldom rises to be mate of a deep-water ship who is,—but I always dreaded a brutal skipper on account of his absolute authority at sea, where there is no redress. I had once been mixed up in an affair concerning the disappearance of one, on a China trader—but no matter. The affair in hand was tempting and I waited developments.

The little mate saw my course and laid his accordingly.

"S'pose you come around about knock-off time. The agents will be along about then—Sauers and Co.; you know them; and I'll fix the thing for you."

"All right," I said, and after a little conversation relating to the merits of various ships, the *Pirate* in particular, I left and made my way back to my lodgings.

I notified my landlord of my proposed voyage, and he was as gracious as could be expected, at the same time expressing some wonderment at the suddenness of my good fortune.

The more I thought of the matter, the more I felt like trying elsewhere for a berth; but the time flew so rapidly that I found myself on the way to the ship before my misgivings took too strong hold of me.

As I turned down the principal thoroughfare, feeling in a more humorous frame of mind at the many possibilities open to me, I heard a shout. The sound came from a side street, and I looked to see what it meant. Through the door of a saloon a man shot head-long as if fired from a gun. He struck in the gutter and staggered to his feet, where he was immediately surrounded by the crowd of men that had followed him. This promised much in the way of diversion, and I stopped to see what hidden force lurked behind the door of the saloon. As I did so, a short fellow with a great bushy head emerged, struggling with half a dozen men who bore down upon him and tried to surround and seize him. The little man's face was red from exertion and liquor, but when I caught a glimpse of his great squat nose and huge mouth I had no difficulty in recognizing my acquaintance on the *Pirate*. He backed rapidly away from his antagonists, swinging a pair of arms each of which seemed to be fully half a fathom long while every instant he let out a yell that sounded like the bellow of a mad bull. Suddenly he turned and made off down the street at an astonishing pace for one with such short legs, still letting out a yell at every jump.

The men who had set upon him hesitated an instant before they realized he was getting away; then they started after him, shouting and swearing at a great rate. He was up to me in an instant, and as he dashed by I narrowly missed a clip from his hand, which he swung viciously at me as he passed. I saw in a moment he couldn't escape at the rate he was moving, in spite of his tremendous exertions, so I stepped aside to watch him as the crowd rushed past in pursuit.

The little mate's legs were working like the flying pistons of a locomotive, and his bush hair and beard were streaming aft in the breeze as he neared the corner. Suddenly he stopped, turned about, and dashed right into the foremost of the crowd, letting out a screech and swinging his long arms.

"Git out th' way! Th' devil's broke loose an's comin' for ye," he howled as he sent the foremost man to the pavement. "Don't stop me. I ain't got no time to stop. Don't stop a little bumpkin buster what's got business in both hands. Stand away, or I'll run ye down and sink ye," and he tore through the men, who grabbed him and grappled to get him down. In a second he was going up the street again in exactly the opposite direction, having hurled over or dashed aside the fellows who had seized him.

"Soo—oo—a-y!" he bellowed as he passed. Then he rushed to a doorway where stood a boy's bicycle. He jumped upon the saddle with another yell as he pushed the machine before him, and the next instant was whirling down the thoroughfare with the rapidity of an express train, bawling for people to "Stand clear!" In another moment he was out of sight, in a cloud of dust, and his yells fell to a drone in the distance.

I was in no hurry to get down to the dock, so I strolled around the streets for some time. Then, thinking that the little mate had about run himself out, I made my way to the wharf where the *Pirate* lay.

As I drew near the ship, I was aware of a bushy head above her port quarter-rail, and in a moment the little mate, Trunnell, looked over and hailed me. He was smoking so composedly and appeared so cool and satisfied that I could hardly believe it was the same man I had seen running amuck but an hour before.

"Have a good ride?" I asked.

"So, so; 'twas a bit of a thing to do, though I ain't never rid one of them things afore. They wanted me to cough up stuff for the whole crowd. But nary a cough. One or two drinks is about all I can stand; so when I feels good ye don't want to persuade me over much. Come aboard."

He led me below, where we were joined by the "doctor," a good-looking negro, who, having washed up his few dishes and put out the fire in his galley, came aft and assumed an importance in keeping with a cook of an American clipper ship.

We sat in the forward cabin and chatted for a few minutes, becoming better acquainted, and I must say they both acquitted themselves very creditably for members of the after guard of that notorious vessel. But I had learned long ago that there were good men on all ships, and I was not more than ordinarily surprised at my reception.

The forward cabin was arranged as on all American ships of large tonnage,—that is, with the house built upon the main deck, the forward end of which was a passage athwartships to enable one to get out from either side when the vessel was heeled over at a sharp angle. Next came the mates' rooms on either side of two alleyways leading into the forward saloon, and between the alleyways were closets and lockers. The saloon was quite large and had a table fastened to the floor in the centre, where we now sat and awaited the appearance of the agents. Aft of this saloon, and separated from it by a bulkhead, was the captain's cabin and the staterooms for whatever passengers the ship might carry.

While we were talking I heard a hail. Mr. Trunnell, the mate, instantly jumped to his feet and sprang up the companionway aft, his short, stout legs curving well outward, and giving him the rolling motion often noticed in short sailors. In a moment there were sounds of footsteps on deck, and several men started down the companionway.

The first that reached the cabin deck was a large man with a flowing beard and sharp eyes which took in every object in the cabin at a glance. He came into the forward saloon, and the "doctor" stood up to receive him. He took no notice of the cook, however, but looked sharply at me. Then the mate came in with two other men who showed in a hundred ways that they were captains of sailing ships. The large man addressed one of these. He was a short, stout man with sandy hair; he wore thin gold earrings, and his sun-bronzed face showed that he had but recently come ashore.

"If you don't want to take her out, Cole," said the large man, roughly, "say so and be done with it. I can get Thompson."

"There's nothing in it without the freight money. Halve it and it's a go."

"Andrews has the whole of it according to contract."

"But he's jugged."

"He'll need it all the more," put in the other captain, who was one of the agents. "Colonel Fermoy has put the rate as high as he can."

"I'm sorry, colonel," said the stout skipper, turning to the large man. "Halve or nothing."

"All right, then, nothing. Mr. Trunnell," he continued, turning to the mate, "Captain Cole will not take you out in the morning as he promised. I'll send Captain Thompson along this evening, or the first thing in the morning. I suppose you know him, so it won't be necessary for me to come down again. Is this your mate?" And he looked at me.

"Yessir, that's him," said Mr. Trunnell.

"Got your papers with you?" asked the colonel.

I pulled them out of my pocket and laid them upon the table. He glanced at them a moment and then returned them.

"All right; get your dunnage aboard this evening and report at the office at nine o'clock to-night. Eight pounds, hey?"

I almost gasped. Eight pounds for second mate! Five was the rule.

"Aye, aye, sir," I answered.

"Done. Bear a hand, Mr. Trunnell. Jenkinson will have a crew at five in the morning. Good night." And he turned and left, followed by all except the "doctor," who remained with me until they were ashore. Mr. Trunnell came aboard again in a few minutes, and after thanking him for getting me the job I left the ship and went to attend to my affairs before clearing.

I had my "dunnage" sent aboard and then stopped at the office and signed on. After that, the night being young, I strolled along the more frequented streets and said farewell to my few acquaintances.

I arrived at the ship before midnight and found the only man there to be the watchman. Trunnell and the "doctor" had gone uptown, he said, for a last look around. I turned in at the bottom of an empty berth in one of the staterooms and waited for the after guard to turn to.

The mate came aboard about three in the morning, and as there was much to do, he stuck his head into a bucket of water and tried to get clear of the effects of the bad liquor he had taken. The "doctor" followed a little later, and fell asleep on the cabin floor.

"Has the old man turned up?" asked the mate, bawling into my resting place and rousing me.

"Haven't seen any one come aboard," I answered.

"Well, I reckon he'll be alongside in a few minutes; so you better stand by for a call."

While he spoke, the watchman on deck hailed some one, and a moment later a steady tramp sounded along the main deck, and a man came through the port door and into the alleyway.

He hesitated for an instant, while a young man with rosy cheeks and light curly hair followed through the door and halted alongside the first comer.

The stranger was tall and slender, with a long face, and high, sharp features, his nose curving like a parrot's beak over a heavy dark mustache. His face was pale and his skin had the clear look of a man who never is exposed to the sun. But his eyes were the objects that attracted my gaze. They were bright as steel points and looked out from under heavy, straight brows with a quick, restless motion I had observed to belong to men used to sudden and desperate resolves. He advanced into the cabin and scrutinized the surroundings carefully before speaking.

"I suppose you are Mr. Trunnell," he said to me, for I had now arisen and stood in the doorway of the stateroom. His voice was low and distinct, and I noticed it was not unpleasant.

"I have that honor," said the little mate, with drunken gravity, sobering quickly, however, under the stranger's look.

"There are no passengers?" asked the man, as the younger companion opened the door leading into the captain's cabin and gazed within.

"Not a bleeding one, and I'm not sorry for that," said Trunnell; "the old man wasn't built exactly on passenger lines."

"You wouldn't take a couple, then, say for a good snug sum?"

"Well, that's the old man's lay, and I can't say as to the why and wherefore. He'll probably be along in an hour or two at best, for the tug will be alongside in a few minutes. We're cleared, and we'll get to sea as soon as the bloody crimp gets the bleeding windjammers aboard. They ought to be along presently."

"Em-m-m," said the man, and stroked his chin thoughtfully. "He'll be along shortly, will he,—and you are all ready. I think I can hear the tug coming now, hey? Isn't that it?"

"S'pose so," answered the mate.

"Well, just let me insinuate to you politely, my boy, that the sooner you clear, the better;" his voice was low and full of meaning, and he leaned toward the mate in a menacing manner; "and if I have to speak to you more than once, my little friend, you will find out the kind of man Captain Thompson is. Can you rise to that?"

Trunnell shrank from the stranger's look, for he stuck his face right into the mate's, and as he finished he raised his voice to its full volume. The liquor was still in the stout little fellow's head, and he drew back one of his long arms as if about to strike; then quickly recovering himself, he scratched his head and stepped back a pace.

"How the bleeding thunder could I tell you were Captain Thompson, when you come aboard here and ask for a passage?" he demanded. "I meant no disrespect. Not a bit. No, sir, not a bloody bit. I'm here for further orders. Yessir, I'm here for further orders and nothin' else. Sing out and I go."

It was plain that the little bushy-headed fellow was not afraid, for he squared his broad shoulders and stood at attention like a man who has dealt with desperate men and knew how to get along with them. At the same time he knew his position and was careful not to go too far. He was evidently disturbed, however, for the little thin silver rings in his ears shook from either nervousness or the effects of liquor.

The tall man looked keenly at him, and appeared to think. Then he smiled broadly.

"Well, you are a clever little chap, Trunnell," he said; "but for discernment I don't think you'd lay a very straight course, hey? isn't that it? Not a very straight course. But with my help I reckon we'll navigate this ship all right. Who's this?" and he turned toward me.

"That's Mr. Rolling, the second mate. Didn't you meet him at the office? He was there only a couple of hours ago. Just signed on this evening."

"Ah, yes, I see. A new hand, hey? Well, Mr. Rolling, I suppose you know what's expected of you. I don't interfere with my mates after I get to sea. Can you locate the ship and reckon her course?"

I told him I could; and although I did not like the unnautical way this stranger had about him, I was glad to hear that he did not interfere with his mates. If he were some hard skipper the agents had taken at a pinch, it was just as well for him to keep to himself aft, and let his mates stand watch as they should on every high-class ship. The young man, or rather boy, who had come aboard with him, looked at me curiously with a pair of bright blue eyes, while the captain spoke, and appeared to enjoy the interrogation, for he smiled pleasantly.

"Everything is all ready, as I see," the captain continued. "So I'll go to bed awhile until my things come aboard. This young man will be third mate, Mr. Trunnell, and I'll put him under your care. He will go ashore now and see to the trunks. But let me know the minute the crew come down, for I won't wait for anything after that. You can let the tug take the line and be ready to pull us out."

Then the skipper went into the captain's cabin, and we saw him no more for several hours. The young man went back up town, and half an hour later returned with a cab containing a trunk, which was put in the after-cabin. The skipper heard the noise and bade them not reawaken him under any circumstances until the ship was well out at sea.

"If I have to get up and see to our leaving, some one will be sorry for it," he said, in his menacing voice, and Mr. Trunnell was quite content to leave him alone.

At five in the morning the boarding master brought down the men, and a sorry lot of sailors they were. They counted nineteen all told, and half of them could not speak English. I went among them and searched their dunnage for liquor and weapons, and after finding plenty of both, I bundled the entire outfit into the forecastle and let them sort it the best they could, with the result that they all struck a fair average in the way of clothes. Those who were too drunk to be of any use I let alone, and they made a dirty mess of the clean forecastle. The rest I turned to with some energy and soon had our towing gear overhauled.

There was now a considerable crowd collecting on the dock to watch the ship clear, and as it was still too dark to see objects distinctly, I couldn't tell what was taking place in the waist, for I had to attend sharply to the work on the topgallant forecastle. Mr. Trunnell bawled for the tug to pull away, and the ship started to leave the dock.

At that instant a man rushed through the crowd and sprang upon the rail amidships, where, seizing some of the running rigging, he let himself down to the main deck. He looked aft at Mr. Trunnell, and then seeing that the mate had command of the ship, he looked into the forward cabin and came to where I stood bawling out orders to the men who were passing the tow-line outside the rigging. I called to him and asked who he was and what he wanted, and he told me quickly that he was the twentieth man of the crew and had almost got left.

"What?" I asked; "after getting your advance money?" And I smiled as I thought of his chance of getting away without being caught.

"I never welsh, sir," he replied, "and as I signed on, so will I work. I never skinned a ship yet out of sixpence."

"Most remarkable," I sneered; but the fellow had such a frank, open face that I felt sorry afterward. He was a young man and had probably not learned enough about ships to have such delicate scruples. He had a smooth face and looked intelligent, although it was evident that he was not much of a sailor.

"Well, don't stand gaping. Get to work and show what you are made of. Stow those slops of yours and get into a jumper quick. Where's your bag?" I continued.

"I haven't any."

"Well, lay up there and help loose the maintopsail. Don't stand here."

He looked bewildered for a moment and then started up the fore rigging.

"Here, you blazing idiot," I bawled. "What are you about? Don't you know one end of a ship from another?"

The fellow came to me and spoke in a low voice.

"I have never shipped before the mast—only as cook, or steward," he said.

"Well, you infernal beggar, do you mean to say that you've passed yourself off as a seaman or sailor here?" I cried.

He nodded.

"Then, blast you, if I don't make a sailor of you before you get clear of the ship," I said with some emphasis; for the idea of all hands being incapable made me angry, as the ship would be dependent entirely upon the sailors aboard, until we had taught the landsmen something. The whole outfit was such a scurvy lot it made me sick to think of what would happen if it should come on to blow suddenly and we had to shorten down to reefed topsails. The *Pirate* had double topsail yards fore and aft and all the modern improvements for handling canvas; but her yards were tremendous, and to lift either of her courses on the yards would take not less than half a dozen men even in good weather.

The fellow hung about while I dressed him down and told him about what a worthless specimen of humanity he was. Finally I sent him aft to help where he could, and he lent a hand at the braces in the waist under the direction of

Mr. Trunnell, who stood on the break of the poop, with the young third mate beside him, and gave his orders utterly oblivious to the boy's presence.

In a short time we made an offing, and as the pilot was on the tug, we had only to let go the line and stand away on our course. The t'gallant yards were sent up, then the royals sheeted home, and by dint of great effort and plenty of bawling we got the canvas on her fore and aft and trimmed the yards so as to make each one look as if at odds with its fellows, but yet enough to make a fair wind of the gentle southerly breeze. Then we let go the tow-line and stood to the westward, while the little tug gave a parting whistle and went heading away into the rising sun astern.

II

I will say now that when I look back on that morning it is evident there was a lack of discipline or command on board the *Pirate*; but at the time it did not appear to me to be the fact, because the lack of discipline was not apparent in my watch. Trunnell and I divided up the men between us, and I believe I laid down the law pretty plain to the Dagos and Swedes who fell to my lot. They couldn't understand much of what I said, but they could tell something of my meaning when I held up a rope's-end and belaying-pin before their eyes and made certain significant gestures in regard to their manipulation. This may strike the landsman as unnecessary and somewhat brutal; but, before he passes judgment, he should try to take care of a lot of men who are, for a part, a little lower than beasts.

If a man can understand the language you use, he can sometimes be made to pay attention if he has the right kind of men over him, but when he cannot understand and goes to sea with the certain knowledge he is on a hard ship and will probably come to blows in a few minutes, he must have some ocular demonstration of what is coming if he doesn't jump when a mate sings out to him. Often the safety of the entire ship depends upon the quickness with which an order can be carried out, and a man must not hang back when the danger is deadly. He must do as he is told, instantly and without question; if he gets killed—why, there is no great loss, for any owner or skipper can get a crew aboard at any of the large ports of trade. Of course, if he takes a different point of view, the only thing for him to do is to stay on the beach. He must not ship on a sailing packet that is carrying twenty percent more freight than the law allows and is getting from three to four dollars a ton for carrying it some ten or fifteen thousand miles over every kind of ocean between the frigid zones. My men were surly enough, perhaps because they had heard what kind of treatment they should expect; so after I had told them what they must do, I bade them go below and straighten out their dunnage.

Mr. Trunnell, after separating his men from mine, cursed them individually and collectively as everything he could think of, and only stopped to scratch his big bushy head to figure out some new condemnations. While doing this he saw me coming from the port side, and forthwith he told me to take charge of the ship, as he was dead beat out and would have to soak his head again before coming on watch. He smelled horribly of stale liquor, and his eyes were bloodshot. I thought he would be just as well off below, so I made no protest against taking command.

"Ye see, I never am used to it," he said, with a grin. "I can't drink nothin'. Stave me, Rollins, but the first thing I'll be running foul of some of these Dagos, and I don't want a fracas until I see the lay of the old man. He's a queer one for sure, hey? Did you ever see a skipper with such a look? Sech bleeding eyes—an' nose, hey? Like the beak of an old albatross. He hasn't come out to lay the course yet, but let her go. She'll head within half a point of what she's doin' now. Sink me, but I don't believe there's three bloomin' beggars in my watch as can steer the craft, and she's got a new wheel gear on her too. Call me if the old man comes on deck." As he finished he staggered into the door of the forward cabin and made for his room, leaving me in command.

I went aft and saw the lubber's mark holding on west by south, and after being satisfied that the man steering could tell port from starboard, I climbed the steps to the poop and took a good look around. It was a beautiful morning and the sun shone brightly over our quarter-rail. The land behind us stood boldly outlined against the sky, and the lumpy clouds above were rosy with sunlight.

The air was cool, but not too sharp for comfort; the breeze from the southward blew steadily and just sent the tops of the waves to foam, here and there, like white stars appearing and disappearing on the expanse to windward. The *Pirate* lay along on the port tack, and with her skysails to her trucks she made a beautiful sight. Her canvas was snowy white, showing that no money had been spared on her sails. Her spars were all painted or scraped and her standing rigging tarred down to a beautiful blackness. Only on deck and among the ropes of her running gear was shown that sign of untidiness which distinguishes the merchant vessel from the man-of-war.

I managed to get some hands to work on the braces, and finally got the yards trimmed shipshape and in the American fashion. That was, with the lower yards sharp on the back-stays, the topsails a little further aft, the t'gallant a little further still, until the main-skysail was almost touching with its weather leach cutting into the breeze a point or more forward of the weather beam. The fore and aft canvas was trimmed well, and the outer jibs lifted the ship along at a slapping rate. She was evidently fast in spite of her load, and I looked over the side at the foam that was seething past the lee channels in swirls and eddies which gave forth a cheerful hissing sound as they slipped aft at the rate of six knots an hour. The man at the wheel held her easily, and that was a blessing; for nothing is much worse for a mate's discomfort than a wild ship sheering from side to side leaving a wake like the path of some monstrous snake.

When I looked again on the main deck I saw the figure of a man whom I failed to recognize as a member of the ship's company. He was standing near the opening of the after-hatchway, which had not yet been battened down, and his gaze was fixed upon me. He was a broad-shouldered fellow, about the average height, and was dressed in a tight-fitting black coat which reached to his knees. On his head was a skull cap with a long tassel hanging down from its top, and in his mouth was a handsome meerschaum pipe, which hung down by its stem to the middle of his breast. His beard was long and just turning gray, and his eyebrows were heavy and prominent.

I stood staring at the figure, and I must say I never saw a more brutal expression upon a man's face. His large mouth and thick lips appeared to wear a sneering smile, while his eyes twinkled with undisguised amusement. His nose was large and flat like a Hottentot's, and while I gazed at him in astonishment, he raised it in the air and gave forth a snort which apparently meant that he was well satisfied with the way affairs were being carried on aboard the ship and he was consequently amused.

"Here! you man; what the deuce are you doing aboard here?" I asked as I advanced to the break of the poop and stared down at him. He gave another snort, and looked at me with undisguised contempt, but disdained to answer and turned away, going to the lee rail and expectorating over the side. Then he came slowly back across the main deck, while my spleen rose at his superior indifference. I have always been a man of the people, and have fought my way along to whatever position I have held on the comprehensive rule of give and take. Nothing is so offensive to me as the assumption of superiority when backed solely by a man's own conception of his value. Therefore it was in no pleasant tone that I addressed the stranger on his return to the deck beneath me.

"My fine cock," said I, "if you haven't a tongue, you probably have ears, and if you don't want them to feel like the grate-bars of the galley stove, you'll do well to sing out when I speak. Can you rise to that?"

The man looked me squarely in the eyes, and I never saw such a fiendish expression come into a human face as that which gathered in his. "You infernal, impudent—" he began; and here for a moment followed a string of foul oaths from the man's lips, while he passed his hand behind his back and drew forth a long knife. Then without a moment's further hesitation he sprang up the steps to the poop.

The fiendishness of the attack took me off my guard, for I was not prepared for such a serious fracas during the first half hour in command of the deck; but I saw there was little time to lose. There were no belaying-pins handy, so the thing for me was to get in as close as possible and get the fellow's knife.

As he came up the steps, I rushed for him and kicked out with all my strength, when his face was level with my knees. The toe of my heavy shoe caught him solidly in the neck, and he went over backward almost in a complete somersault, landing with a crash upon the main deck just outside the window of Mr. Trunnell's room. He was stunned by the fall, and I hastened down to seize him before he could recover. Just as I gained the main deck, however, he gave a snort and started to his feet. Then he let out a yell like a madman and closed with me, my right hand luckily reaching his wrist below the knife.

It was up and down, and all over the deck for a time, the men crowding aft around us, but fearing to take a hand. The fellow had enormous strength, and the way he made that knife hand jump and twist gave me all I could do to keep fast to it. Soon I found I was losing ground, and he noted the fact, exerting himself more and more as he found me failing. Then it dawned upon me that I was in a bad fix, and I tried to think quickly for some means to save myself. In another mad struggle he would wrench himself clear, and his ugly look told me plainly how much mercy I could expect. I gave one last despairing grip on his wrist as he tore wildly about, and then I felt his arm slip clear of my fingers, and I waited for the stroke with my left arm drawn up to stop its force as far as possible. I could almost feel the sting of the steel in my tense nerves, when something suddenly caught me around the middle and pressed me with great force against my enemy. His face was almost against mine, but his arms were pinioned to his sides, powerless, and then I was aware that we both were encircled by the ape-like arms of the mate, Mr. Trunnell. How the little fellow held on was a marvel. He braced his short legs wide apart, and giving a hug that almost took the breath out of me, bawled lustily for some man to pass a lashing.

Suddenly a man rushed aft and passed a line around the stranger, and I saw that the young landlubber to whom, earlier in the morning, I had been so harsh was a man to be depended on. The young fellow tied my enemy up in short order, although the knots he used would not have done any credit to a sailor. But I was more than thankful when I had a chance to wring the long knife out of the murderous stranger's hand, and I spoke out to the smooth-faced fellow. "You'll do, my boy, even if you don't know a yard from a main-brace bumpkin. Pass a line around his legs and stuff a swab into his mouth if he don't stop swearing."

"Steady," said Trunnell, "none of that," as the swab was being brought up. "But, Captain Andrews, if you don't belay your tongue we'll have to do something." And the little mate squared his shoulders, and gazed calmly down upon the prostrate stranger who foamed at the mouth with impotent fury.

"So," I said, "this is the ruffian who jumped his bail and is aboard here on the sneak? I reckon we'll tack ship and stand back again to put him where he belongs."

I was breathing heavily from the fight, and stood leaning against the cabin to recover, while Mr. Trunnell and the fellow Jim, who had helped tie the skipper up, appeared to be in doubt how to proceed. The noise of the scuffle and our conversation had aroused the captain in the cabin, and as I finished speaking he came to the break of the poop and looked down on the main deck. I was aware of his hooked nose and strange, glinting eyes almost before I turned, as he spoke. He placed his foot upon the rail and gave a dry cough.

"I reckon there ain't any call to tack ship," he said slowly; "a pair of irons'll do the rest. Jest clap them on him, hand and foot, Mr. Rolling, and then rivet him to the deck away up forrads. If he don't stow that bazoo of his, you might ram the end of a handspike in his mouth and see if he'll bite."

"Who are you, you molly-hawk, to give orders aboard here?" roared Andrews, from where he lay on deck. "What's happened, Trunnell, when a swivel-eyed idiot with a beak like an albatross stands on the poop and talks to me like this?"

"He's Captain Thompson, in command, owing to the little—the little fracas you was mixed into last v'yage. We didn't exactly expect to have ye this trip, sir," said the mate.

"Well, I'm here, ain't I? Sing out, can't you see me? Has your hair struck in and tickled your brain so you don't know who's boss aboard here? Who's this galoot you've just kept from being ripped to ribbons? I'll settle matters with you later on for meddling in this affair, you kelp-haired sea-pig. Sink you, Trunnell; I never expected you to turn rusty like the miserable swab you are."

"Don't you think it would be best to stand away for port again, sir?" said the fellow Jim, looking sharply at the skipper on the poop as he spoke, and then to myself and Trunnell.

"We don't keer for your suggestions, young feller," said the skipper, leaning over the rail above us. "When there's any orders to be given, I'll attend to matters myself." He spoke in a low, even tone, and his eyes seemed to focus to two sharp, bright points at the sailor, making his great beak-like nose more prominent.

"Cast me adrift, Trunnell," commanded the ruffian Andrews, with an oath. "I'm a-going to kill that lubber you've got for mate anyhow, and it might as well be done at once as any other time. We'll settle the matter about who's skipper afterward."

"I hears ye well enough, Cap'n Andrews," said Trunnell; "but I ain't eggzactly clear in my mind as to how ye have authority aboard. If I was, I'd cast ye adrift in spite o' the whole crowd, an' ye could rip an' cut to your bloody heart's content. Ye know I'd back ye if 'twas all right and proper; but I never disobeyed an order yet, and stave me, I never will. I don't care who gives it so long as he has the right."

"Spoken like a man an' a sailor," came the sudden sharp tones of the skipper on the poop; and as I looked, the skipper drew forth a watch in one hand and a long revolver in the other, which clicked to readiness as it came in a line between his eye and the body of Andrews. "You have just a few seconds less than a minute to get that fellow forrads and out of the way," he said slowly, as if counting his words. I made no movement to drag the ruffian away, for at that minute I would have offered no objection whatever to seeing the skipper make a target of him; but Trunnell and the sailor Jim instantly seized Andrews, while he cursed the captain and dared him shoot. He struggled vainly to get free of his lashings, but the little bushy-headed mate tucked him under his arm, while Jim took his feet, and the crowd of gaping men broke away as they went forward.

III

After I had recovered from my somewhat violent exertions, and bound up the slight cut that Andrews had made in my hand with his knife, eight bells had struck, and the steward brought aft the cabin hash. The skipper went below, and Trunnell and I followed.

Captain Thompson seated himself at the head of the table and signed for us to take our places; then it suddenly occurred to me that I was only second mate, and consequently did not rate the captain's table. Trunnell noticed my hesitation, but said nothing, and the skipper fell to with such a hearty good will that he appeared to entirely forget my presence. I hastily made some excuse to get back on deck, and the little, bushy-headed mate smiled and nodded approvingly at me as I went up the alleyway forward. I was much pleased at this delicate hint on his part, for many mates would have made uncalled-for remarks at such a blunder. It showed me that the little giant who could keep me from being carved to rat-line stuff could be civil also.

I was much taken with him owing to what had happened, and I looked down at him as he ate, for I could see him very well as I stood near the mizzen on the port side of the cabin skylight. The glass of the hatch was raised to let the cabin air, and I watched the bushy head beneath, with its aggressive beard bending over the dirty table-cloth. The large squat nose seemed to sniff the good grub as the steward served the fresh beef, and Trunnell made ready with his knife.

He laid the blade on his plate and heaped several large chunks of the meat and potatoes upon it. Then he dropped his chin and seemed to shut his eyes as he carefully conveyed the load to his mouth, drawing the steel quickly through his thick lips without spilling more than a commensurate amount of the stuff upon his beard, and injuring himself in no way whatever. The quick jerk with which he slipped the steel clear so as to have it ready for another load made me a trifle nervous; but it was evident that he was not a novice at eating. Indeed, the skipper appeared to admire his dexterity, for I saw his small, glinting eyes look sharply from the little fellow to the boyish third officer who sat to starboard.

"Never had no call for a fork, eh?" said he, after watching the mate apparently come within an inch of cutting his head in two.

"Nope," said Trunnell.

They ate in silence for some minutes.

"I like to see a fellow what can make out with the fewest tools. Tools are good enough for mechanics; a bit an' a bar'll do for a man. Ever been to New York?"

"Nope," said Trunnell.

There was a moment's silence.

"I might 'a' knowed that," said the skipper, as if to himself.

Trunnell appeared to sniff sarcasm.

"Oh, I've been to one or two places in my time," said he. "There ain't nothin' remarkable about New York except the animals, and I don't keer fer those."

"Whatchermean?"

"Oh, I was closte into the beach off Sandy Hook onct when we was tryin' to get to the south'ard, an' I see an eliphint about a hundred feet high on the island acrost the bay. There was a feller aboard as said they had cows there just as big what give milk. I wouldn't have believed him, but fer the fact that there ware the eliphint before my eyes."

"Stuffed, man,—he was stuffed," explained the captain.

"Stuffed or no; there he ware," persisted Trunnell. "He would 'a' been no bigger stuffed than alive. 'Tain't likely they could 'a' stretched his hide more'n a foot."

The skipper gave the third mate a sly look, and his nose worked busily like a parrot's beak for a few minutes.

"You believe lots o' things, eh?" said he, while his nose worked and wrinkled in amusement.

"I believe in pretty much all I sees an' some little I hears," said Trunnell, dryly.

"'Specially in eliphints, eh?—a hundred feet high?"

"But not in argufying over facts," retorted Trunnell. "No, sink me, when I finds I'm argufying agin the world,—agin facts,—I tries to give in some and let the world get the best o' the argument. I've opinions the same as you have, but when they don't agree with the rest o' the world, do I go snortin' around a-tryin' to show how the world is wrong an' I am right? Sink me if I do. No, I tries to let the other fellow have a show. I may be right, but if I sees the world is agin me, I—"

"Right ye are, Trunnell. Spoken O.K." said the skipper. "I like to see a man what believes in a few things—even if they's eliphints. What do you think of the fellow forrads? Do you believe in him to any extent?"

The third mate appeared much amused at the conversation, but did not speak. He was a remarkably good-looking young fellow, and I noted the fact at the time.

Trunnell did not answer the last remark, but held himself very straight in his chair.

"Do you believe much in the fellow who was skipper, especially after his tryin' to carve Mr. Rolling?"

"I believe him a good sailor," said Trunnell, stiffening up.

"Ye don't say?" said the skipper.

"I never critisizez my officers," said Trunnell; and after that the skipper let him alone.

I was pleased with Trunnell. His philosophy was all right, and I believed from that time he was an honest man. Things began to look a little brighter, and in spite of an aversion to the skipper which had begun to creep upon me, I now saw that he was an observing fellow, and was quick to know the value of men. I didn't like his allusion to a bit and bar for a man, but thought little about the matter. In a short time Trunnell relieved me, and I went below with the carpenter and steward to our mess.

The carpenter was a young Irishman, shipped for the first time. This was the first time I had been to sea with a ship carpenter who was not either a Russian, a Finn, or a Swede. The steward was a little mulatto, who announced, as he sat down, after bringing in the hash, that he was bloody glad he was an Englishman, and looked at me for approval.

This was to show that he did not approve of the scene he had witnessed on the main deck in the morning, and I accepted it as a token of friendship.

"'Tis cold th' owld man thinks it is, whin he has th' skylight wide open," said Chips, looking up at the form of Trunnell, who stood on the poop. There was a strange light in the young fellow's eye as he spoke, as if he wished to impart some information, and had not quite determined upon the time and place. I took the hint and smiled knowingly, and then glanced askance at the steward.

"Faith, he's all right," blurted out Chips; "his skin is a little off th' color av roses, but his heart is white. We're wid ye, see?"

"With me for what?" I asked.

"Anything," he replied. "To go back, to go ahead. There's a fellow forrads who says go back while ye may."

"An' it's bloody good advice," said the steward, in a low tone.

"I'm not exactly in command aboard here," I said.

"D'ye know who is?" asked Chips.

"His name is Thompson, I believe," I answered coldly, for I did not approve of this sudden criticism of the skipper, much as I disliked his style.

"See here, mate, ye needn't think we're fer sayin' agin the old man, so hark ye, don't take it hard like. Did ye iver hear tell av a sailorman a-callin' a line a 'rope' or a bloomin' hooker like this a 'boat'? No, sir, ye can lay to it he's niver had a ship before; an' so says Jim Potts, the same as passed th' line fer ye this mornin'. Kin I pass ye the junk? It's sort o' snifty fer new slush, but I don't complain."

"What's the matter with the meat?" I asked, glad to change the conversation.

"Jest sort o' snifty."

"That's what," corroborated the steward, looking at me. "Jest sort o' smelly like fer new junk."

"What has Jim Potts got against the old man?" I asked. "You said he didn't believe the skipper had been in a ship before."

"Nothin' I knows of, 'cept he was hot fer turnin' back this mornin' an' tried to get th' men to back him in comin' aft."

"Do you mean it's mutiny?"

"Lord, no; jest to blandander ye inter tackin' ship. He most persuaded Mr. Trunnell, an' wid ye too, 'twould ha' been no mutiny to override the new skipper, an' land th' other in th' caboose."

Much as I would have liked to get ashore again, I knew there was no immediate prospect of it. The skipper would not hear of any such thing. As for Trunnell acting against orders, I knew from what I had seen of this sturdy little fellow he would obey implicitly any directions given him, and at any cost. There was no help for it now. We would be out for months with the ruffian skipper forward and the strange one aft. I said nothing more to the carpenter or steward, for it was evident that there had been some strong arguments used by Jim Potts against the regularity of the ship's company. The more I thought of this, the more I was astonished, for the young landsman was not forced to come out in the ship, and had almost been left, as it was. I went on deck in a troubled frame of mind, and determined to keep my eye on every one who approached me, for the voyage had the worst possible beginning.

There was much to be done about the main deck, so I busied myself the entire afternoon getting the running gear cleared up and coiled down shipshape. The skipper stood near the break of the poop much of the time, but gave no orders, and I noticed that Jim the sailor, or landsman, kept away from his vicinity. Sometimes it seemed as though the captain would follow his movements about the deck forward with his keen eyes.

It was Trunnell's dog-watch that evening, and by the time the bells struck the vessel was running along to the westward under royals, with the southerly breeze freshening on her beam. She was a handsome ship. Her long, tapering spars rose towering into the semi-gloom overhead, and the great fabric of stretched canvas seemed like a huge cloud resting upon a dark, floating object on the surface of the sea, which was carried along rapidly with it, brushing the foam to either side with a roaring, rattling, seething, musical noise. At least, this is the picture she presented from the forecastle head looking aft. Her great main yard swung far over the water to leeward, and the huge bellying courses, setting tight as a drumhead with the pressure, sent the roaring of the bow-wave back in a deep booming echo, until the air was full of vibration from the taut fabric. All around, the horizon was melted into haze, but the stars were glinting overhead in promise of a clear night.

I left the forecastle head and came down on the main deck. Here the six-foot bulwarks shut off the view to windward, but little of the cool evening breeze. The men on watch were grouped about the waist, sitting on the combings of the after-hatch, or walking fore and aft in the gangways to keep the blood stirring. All had pea coats or mufflers over their jumpers, for the air was frosty. The "doctor" had washed up his pots and coppers for the evening, and had made his way toward the carpenter's room in the forward house, where a light shone through the crack of the door.

On nearly all American ships the carpenter is rated as an officer, but does not have to stand watch, turning out only during the day-time or when all hands are called in cases of emergency. The cook, or "doctor," as he is called, also turns in for the night, as do the steward and cabin boys; the steward, however, generally has a stateroom aft near those of the mates, while the "doctor" bunks next his galley. The carpenter having permission to burn a light, usually turns his shop or bunk-room into a meeting place for those officers who rate the distinction of being above the ordinary sailor. Here one can always hear the news aboard ships where the discipline is not too rigid; for the mates, bos'n, "doctor," steward, and sometimes even the quartermasters, enjoy his hospitality.

Trunnell was on the poop, and the captain was below. I had a chance to get a little better insight into the natures of my shipmates if I could join in their conversation, or even listen to it for a while. My position as second mate was not too exalted to prohibit terms of intimacy with the carpenter, or, for that matter, even the bos'n.

I took a last look to windward, over the cold southern ocean, where the sharp evening breeze was rolling the short seas into little patches of white. The horizon was clear, and there was no prospect for some time of any sudden call to shorten sail. The sky was a perfect blue vault in which the stars were twinkling, while the red of the recent sunset held fair on the jibboom end, showing that the quartermaster at the wheel knew his business. I edged toward the door of the house, and then seeing that my actions were not creating too much notice from the poop, I slid back the white panel and entered. The fog from damp clothes and bad tobacco hung heavy in the close air and made a blue halo about the little swinging lamp on the bulkhead. Chips, who was sitting on his sea-chest, waved his hand in welcome, and the "doctor" nodded and showed his white teeth. The bos'n was holding forth in full swing in an argument with one of the quartermasters, and Jim, the fellow I noticed in the morning, was listening. He arose as I entered, as also did the quartermaster, but the rest remained seated. I waved my hand in friendly acknowledgment and lit my pipe at the lamp, while they reseated themselves.

"Yah, good mornin' to ye—if it ain't too late in the day," said Chips. "Sit ye down an' listen to me song, for 'tis a quare ship, an' th' only thing to do is to square our luck wid a good song. Cast loose, bos'n."

We were all new men to the vessel except the carpenter, and had never even sailed in the same ship before on any previous voyage. Yet the bos'n "cast loose" without further orders, and the "doctor" joined in with his bass voice. Then Chips and the rest bawled forth to the tune of "Blow a man down," and all the dismal prospect of the future in an overloaded ship, with bad food and a queer skipper, was lost in the effort of each one trying to out-bellow his neighbor. Sailors are a strange set. It takes mighty little to please one at times when he should, with reason, be sad; while, again, when everything is fair, nothing will satisfy his whims.

When the yarn spinning and singing were over, I turned out for my first watch well pleased with my shipmates.

IV

During the following days all hands were so busy bending new sails and reeving running gear for our turn of the Cape that there was little time for anything else. Much of this work could have been avoided had the ship been under better command when she cleared, but Trunnell had no authority to do anything, and the agents were waiting until the skipper took command and could attend to the necessary overhauling.

At meals I saw little of either Trunnell or Captain Thompson and his third mate, but in the short hours of the dog-watch in the evening I had a chance to talk with them upon other subjects than those relating immediately to the running of the ship.

The dog-watch is the short watch between six and eight o'clock in the evening. This is made short to keep one watch from turning to at any regular time and consequently getting all the disagreeable work to be done during those hours. For instance, if one watch had to be on deck every night from twelve until four in the morning, it would mean that the other watch would be on deck from four to eight, and consequently would have to do all the washing down of decks and other work which occurs upon every regulated ship before breakfast. So the dog-watch divides a four-hour watch and is served alternately. As second mate I had access to the poop and could come aft on the weather side like any officer, all sailors, of course, being made to go to leeward.

Trunnell grew to be confidential, and we often discoursed upon many subjects during the hours after supper; for there was little time to turn in when not on dog-watch, and the skipper allowed me aft with much more freedom than many second mates get. He seldom ventured to join in the conversations, except when discussing shore topics, for his ignorance of things nautical was becoming more and more apparent to me every day, and he saw it. I wondered vaguely how he ever managed to get command of the ship, and set the reason down to the fact that the agents were glad enough to get any one to take her out. He, however, checked up Trunnell's sights every day and commented upon their accuracy with much freedom, finding fault often, and cautioning him to be more careful in the future. This somewhat perplexed the mate, as he always made his reckoning by rule of thumb, and could no more change his method than work out a problem in trigonometry. The third mate, on the other hand, was quite shy. I noticed what I had failed to note before, and that was the peculiar feminine tone of his voice and manner. He never swung his hands or lounged along the deck like a man used to the sea, and as the regulations call for at least two years' sea experience certified to by some reputable skipper before a mate's certificate is issued, this struck me as strange. Besides, he walked with a short mincing step that failed to swing his rather broad hips, and his knees were well set back at each stride, that went to show more conclusively than anything else that he was not used to a heaving deck. An old sailor, or a young one either, for that matter, will bend his knees to catch the roll and not try to walk like a soldier.

One evening after we had been out about a week, Trunnell and I happened to be standing aft near the taffrail looking up at a royal preventer stay.

"D'ye know what th' old man called this cleat?" asked Trunnell, pointing to where it had been made fast.

"No," said I. "What did he call it?"

"A timber noggin."

"Well, that don't prove there is anything wrong with him, does it?" I queried.

"Either that or the timber noggins has changed summat in character since I seen them last," said Trunnell. "What in Davy Jones would a skipper of a ship call a cleat a timber noggin for unless he didn't know no better?"

"A man might or might not have many reasons for calling a cleat a timber noggin besides that of not knowing any better than to do so," I responded. "For instance—"

But Trunnell cut me short. "No, Mr. Rolling, there ain't no use disguising the fact any more, this skipper don't know nothin' about a ship. You'll find that out before we get to the west'ard o' the Agullas. Mind ye, I ain't making no criticism o' the old man. I never does that to no superior officer, but when a man tells me to do the things he does, it stands to reason that we've got an old man aboard here who's been in a ship for the first time as officer."

I agreed with him, and he was much pleased.

"A man what finds fault an' criticises everybody above him is always a failure, Mr. Rolling," he went on. "Yes, sir, the faultfinder is always a failure. An' the reason so many sailors find fault all the time is because they is failures. I am tryin' not to find fault with the skipper, but to pint out that we're in for some rough times if things don't change aboard in the sailorin' line afore we gets to the west'ard o' the Agullas. Sink me, if that ain't so, for here we is without half the sails bent an' no new braces, nothin' but two-year-old manila stuff what's wore clean through. Them topsails look good enough, but they is as rotten with the lime in them as if they was burned. No, sir, I ain't makin' no criticism, but I burns within when I think of the trouble a few dollars would save. Yes, sir, I burns within."

Mr. Trunnell here spat profusely to leeward and walked athwartships for some moments without further remark. The third mate came on deck and stood near the lee mizzen rigging, looking forward at the foam swirling from the bends and drifting aft alongside at a rapid rate. The phosphorus shone brilliantly in the water, and the wake of the ship was like a path of molten metal, for the night was quite dark and the heavy banks of clouds which had been making steadily to the westward over-spread the sky. It was nearly time for the southwest monsoon to shift, and with this change would likely follow a spell o' weather, as Trunnell chose to put it. The third mate had never given an order since he had come aboard, and I noticed Trunnell's sly wink as he glanced in the direction of the mizzen.

"Mr. Rolling," said he, "wimmen have been my ruin. Yes, sir, wimmen have been my ruin, an' I'm that scared o' them I can raise them afore their topmast is above the horizon. Sink me, if that ain't one." And he leered at the figure of the third mate, whom we knew as Mr. Bell.

"What would a woman be doing here as third mate?" I asked; for although I had come to the same conclusion some days before, I had said nothing to any one about it.

"That's the old man's affair," said Trunnell; "it may be his wife, or it may be his daughter, but any one can see that the fellow's pants are entirely too big in the heft for a man. An' his voice! Sink me, Rolling, but you never hearn tell of a man or boy pipin' so soft like. Why, it skeers me to listen to it. It's just like—but no matter."

"Like what?" I suggested gently, hoping much.

But it was of no use. Trunnell looked at me queerly for a moment as if undecided to give me his confidence. Then he resumed his walk athwart the deck, and I went forward to the break of the poop and took a look at the head sails.

The night was growing darker, and the breeze was dying slowly, and I wondered why the skipper had not come on deck to take a look around. He was usually on hand during the earlier hours of evening.

I reached the side of the third officer, and stood silently gazing at the canvas which shone dimly through the gathering gloom. As we had always been separated on account of being in different watches, I had never addressed the third mate before save in a general way when reporting the ship's duties aft.

"Pretty dark night, hey?" I ventured.

The third officer looked hard at me for the space of a minute, during which time his face underwent many changes of expression. Then he answered in a smooth, even tone.

"Sorter," said he.

This was hardly what I expected, so I ventured again.

"Looks as if we might have a spell o' weather, hey? The wind's falling all the time, and if it keeps on, we'll have a calm night without a draught of air."

"What do you mean by a ca'm night without a draft of air?" asked the young fellow, in a superior tone, while at the same time I detected a smile lurking about the corners of his eyes.

If there's one thing I hate to see in a young fellow, it is the desire to make fun of a superior's conversation. Being an American sailor, I had little use for *r*'s in every word which held an *a* but I had no objection to any one else talking the way they wished. I was somewhat doubtful just how to sit upon this nebulous third mate, so I began easily.

"Do you know," said I, "there are a great many young fellows going out in ships as officers when they could be of much more benefit to people generally if they stayed home and helped their mothers to 'bark cark,' or do other little things around the nursery or kitchen."

As I finished I thought I heard some one swear fiercely in a low tone. I looked over the poop rail down to the main deck beneath, but saw no one near. The third officer seemed to be lost in thought for a moment.

"It isn't good to be too clever," said he, in the tone which was unmistakably a woman's. "When a person is good at baking cake, or 'barking cark,' as you choose to call it, the sea is a good place for them. They can look out for those who haven't sense enough to perform the function."

I had a strong notion to ask him outright if he was fitted to perform the function, but his superior air and the feeling that I might make a mistake after all and incur the displeasure of the beak-nosed skipper deterred me. But I was almost certain that our third mate was a woman.

We remained standing together in the night for a few moments while neither spoke. My advances had not received the favorable acknowledgment I had expected, and there was a distinctly disagreeable feeling creeping upon me while in this neutral presence. I was young and hot-headed, so I spoke accordingly before leaving the field, or rather deck, in retreat.

"I wish you had the distinction of belonging to the port watch."

"Why?"

"I think I might strengthen your powers of discernment regarding the relative positions of second and third mates."

"We'll see who has the better insight in regard to the matter without my being bored to that extent," said the third officer in his softest tones, and again I fancied I heard the voice of a man swearing fiercely in a low voice as if to himself. Then I turned and went aft.

"It's something queer," said Trunnell, shaking his great shaggy head and glancing toward the break of the poop. A step sounded on the companion ladder, and the skipper came on deck.

"Pretty dark, hey?" he said, and his quick eyes took in both Trunnell and myself comprehensively.

"Looks like we might have a spell o' weather if the wind keeps fallin'," observed Trunnell.

"Well, I don't suppose a dark night is any worse than a bright one, and I call to mind many a time I'd give something to see it a bit blacker. Do you know where you're at?"

"She's headin' about the same, but if ye don't mind, I'll be gettin' her down gradual like to her torps'ls if the glass keeps a-fallin'. Short commons, says I, on the edge o' the monsoon."

"Short it is, my boy. Get her down low. The more she looks like you, the better she'll do, hey? What d'you think of that, Mr. Rolling? The shorter the longer, the longer the shorter—see? The sooner the quicker, eh? Supposen the question was asked you, Mr. Rolling, what'd you say, hey? Why is Mr. Trunnell like a lady's bouquet, hey? Why is the little man like a bunch of flowers? Don't insult him, Mr. Rolling. The sanitary outfit of the cabin is all right. 'Tain't that. No, split me, it ain't that. Think a minute."

Trunnell walked to and fro without a word, while the captain grinned. The fellow at the wheel, Bill Spielgen, a square-cut man with an angular face and enormous hands, stared sullenly into the binnacle.

"It's because he's a daisy," rapped out the skipper. "That's it, Mr. Rolling, he's a daisy, ha, ha, ha! Split me, if he ain't, ho, ho, ho! Shorten her down, Trunnell; you're a daisy, and no mistake."

There was a distinct smell of liquor in the light breeze, and as the skipper came within the glare of the binnacle lamp I could see he was well set up. Trunnell went to the break of the poop and called out for the watch to clew down the fore and mizzen skysails. He was much upset at the skipper's talk, but knew better than to show it. The captain now turned his attention to the man at the wheel,

"How d'you head, Bill?" said he.

"West b' no'the," said Bill.

The skipper came to the wheel and stuck his lean face close to the quartermaster's. His glinting eyes grew to two little points and his hooked nose wrinkled on the sides as he showed his teeth while he drawled in a snarling tone:—

"D'you set up for a wit, Bill, that you joke with your captain, hey? Is that it, you square-toed, lantern-jawed swab? Would you like me to rip you up the back, or lam some of the dirt out of your hide, hey? Is that it? Don't make jokes at your captain, Bill. It's bad business."

Then he went on in a more conciliating tone:—

"Just remember that I'm a knight of a round table, or square one either, for that matter, while I'm aboard this boat, and if you forget to mention my title of 'Sir,' every time you speak of me, you'll want to get your hide sewed on tight."

"I beg pardon, sir," said Bill, taking a fresh grip upon the spokes with his great hands.

"That's right, my son; you're a beggar aboard this here boat. Don't aspire to anything else."

"Aye, aye, sir," said the quartermaster.

"And now that you've got to your bearings, as Trunnell would say, I'll tell you a little story about a man who lost a pet dog called Willie."

I saw that it was high time for me to get forward, and slipped away. I turned in ready for a call, thinking that perhaps Trunnell was right in regard to our future prospects in the South Atlantic.

V

When I turned out for the mid-watch that night, Trunnell met me at the door of the forward cabin. It was pitch dark on deck, and the wind had died away almost entirely. The canvas had been rolled up, as it had begun to slat heavily against the masts with the heave from a long, quick swell that ran rapidly from the southward. The running gear was not new, and Trunnell was a careful mate, so the ship was down to her upper topsails on the fore and mizzen and a main t'gallant on mainmast, the courses fore and after being clewed up and left hanging.

"He's out for trouble to-night," said the little mate. "Blast him if he ain't touching the boose again."

"Who, the skipper?" I asked.

"He's been below twice during the watch, an' each time he's gettin' worse an' worse. There he comes now to the edge of the poop."

I looked and saw our old man rolling easily across the deck to the poop rail. There he stopped and bawled out loudly,—

"Lay aft to the main-brace."

The men on watch hesitated a moment and then came crowding aft and began to cast off the weather-brace from its belaying-pin.

It was so dark I couldn't see how many men were there, but I noticed Bill the quartermaster, and as I stood waiting to see what would happen, a little sailor by the name of Johnson, who had a face like a monkey's and legs set wide apart, so they never touched clear up to his waist, spoke out to a long, lean Yankee man who jostled me in the darkness.

"Don't pull a pound on the bleeding line. The old cock's drunk, an' we ain't here to be hazed around decks like a pack o' damned boys."

The skipper, however, didn't wait to see if his order was carried out, but came down from the poop and asked for Trunnell and myself. We went with him into the forward cabin, and he motioned us to sit down.

"Did you ever see such a lot o' confounded fools?" he said. "Here I calls for to take a pull in the main-brace, and the whole crowd of duff-eaters come layin' aft as if the skipper of a ship should blow them all off to drinks. Blast me, Trunnell, I'd 'a' thought you'd get them into better discipline. It's come to a fine state o' things when the whole crew turns to every time I get thirsty. But never mind, sing out as you says, and tell the steward what kind o' pisin you'll mix with your blood current. Mine's the same old thing."

"It's my watch below now," said Mr. Trunnell, "an' if you'll excuse me, I'll turn in. The third mate's gone below some time ago."

"Oh, the boat's all right. It's dead calm, and she can't hurt herself floating around this ocean," said the old man. "You can take a drink before you go. Steward! Ahoy there, steward!"

"Yessir," said that active mulatto, springing out of his cabin. "Yessir; I hears yo', cap'n."

"What'll you have?" asked Thompson, addressing the mate.

Trunnell scratched his big bushy head a moment, and then suggested that a bottle of the ginger pop which the steward had in the pantry would do for him.

"Hell'n blazes, man, take a drink o' something," cried Thompson, turning upon him with his fierce eyes. "What's the matter with you?"

"Nothin', only I drinks what I drinks or else I don't drink at all," said Trunnell. "Ye asked me what I'd have, an' I says it."

"All right, Shorty," said Thompson, in mock gravity. "You drinks what you drinks. What's yours, Rolling?"

"As I've just turned to, a little soda will do for me," I answered. "I'd rather take my grog in the morning at regular hours."

Thompson let his hand fall upon the table with a crash, and then sat motionless, looking from one to the other, his long, beak-like nose twitching convulsively.

"Steward," said he, with a nasal drawl which made his hooked nose wrinkle, "get Mr. Trunnell a drink o' ginger pop, or milk, if he prefers it, and then, steward, you may get Mr. Rolling a drink o' sody water. It's hot, but I reckon it'll fizz."

"Yessah. What's yourn, cap'n?"

"You don't think there's a priest aboard here, do you, steward, hey?"

"No, sah, 'tain't likely, but I ken find out, sah. Shall I get yo' drink fust, sah?"

"Well, I dunno, I dunno, steward; I can't think what I kin take what won't offend these gentlemen. You might see first if there's a priest, an' if you find one you can bring me a pint or so o' holy water. If it's too strong for you," said he, turning toward Trunnell and myself, "I can get the steward to dilute it for me, hey?"

Trunnell made no remark at this. The steward brought in our drinks and informed the skipper loudly that there was no one in the crew who had held holy orders.

"Never mind, then, steward," said Thompson. "I'll wait till it rains and get it fresh from heaven."

In a moment Trunnell rose and went into his room with a rough "good night." Thompson arose and passed through the door in the bulkhead, and I went on deck to take charge.

The night was quiet, and I leaned over the poop rail, looking into the water alongside, which appeared as black as ink. The *Pirate* had little or no headway, for it was now dead calm. Forward at the bends a sudden flare of phosphorescent fire would burn for a moment alongside when the heavy ship rolled deeply and soused her channels under. The southerly swell seemed to roll quickly as if there were something behind it, and the topsails slatted fore and aft with loud flaps as they backed and filled with the motion. It was a bad night for wearing out gear, and I was glad Trunnell had rolled up the lighter canvas. Chafing gear had been scarce aboard, and nothing is so aggravating to a mate as to have his cotton or spars cut by useless rolling in a quiet seaway. If sails can be kept full of wind, they will last well enough with care; but let them slat for a few days, and there is more useless wear than would take place in a month of ordinary weather, with no headway to pay for it.

While I looked into the dark water I noticed a long thin streak of fire moving slowly alongside. It wavered and snaked along, growing brighter at times and then dying out almost completely. Suddenly it turned at the fore channels and came slowly aft. I looked harder at the black surface below me and tried to see what caused the disturbance. In an instant I beheld a huge shadow, blacker than the surrounding water, outlined faintly with the phosphorescent glow. It was between twenty and thirty feet in length, and had the form of a shark. The grim monster swam slowly aft and rounded the stern, then sank slowly out of sight into the blackness beneath.

There is something so uncanny in the silent watchfulness of these giants of the deep that a sailor always feels unpleasantly disposed toward them. I thought how ghastly would be the ending of any one who should get overboard that night. The sudden splash, the warm water about the body, and the heads of the fellows at the rail starting to pull the unfortunate aboard. Then the sudden grisly clutch from below, and the dragging down out of sight and sound forever.

I began to actually reckon the amount of arsenic I should put into a chunk of beef to trick the giant at his last meal.

"Sharp lightning on port bow, sir," came the news from the forward; for, although I was supposed to be able to see well enough, I had taught the men of my watch to sing out at everything unusual, more to be certain that they were awake than anything else.

I looked up from the black depths and my unpleasant reflections, and gazed to the southward. As I did so, several sharp flashes showed upon the dark horizon. It looked as if something were raising fast, and I stepped below a moment to see the glass. It was down to twenty-eight. Going on deck at once, I bawled for the watch to clew down the main-topgallantsail. In a moment the men were swarming up the main rigging, and the sail was let go by the run, the yard settling nicely, while the clews, buntlines, and leachlines were hauled down in unison.

"Mizzen topsail!" I cried.

The watch came up the poop ladders with a rush and tramping of feet that sounded ominously loud for the work on so quiet a night. The yelling of the men at the braces coupled with the tramping aroused Captain Thompson in spite of his liquor, and he came up the after-companion to see what was the matter.

"Hey, there, hey!" he bawled. "What are you doing, Rolling? Are you coming to an anchor already? Have I been asleep six months, and is this the Breakwater ahead? No? Well, do you expect to get to port without canvas on the ship? Split me, but I thought you knew how to sail a boat when you signed on as mate. Don't come any of these grandmother tricks on me, hey? I won't have it. Don't make a fool of yourself before these men. Get that topsail up again quicker'n hell can scorch a feather, or I'll be taking a hand, see! I'll be taking a hand. Jump lively, you dogs!" he roared, as he finished.

The topsail was swayed up again, the men silent and sullen with this extra work. Then came the order for the t'gallantsail, and by the time that was mastheaded, the skipper followed with orders for royals, fore and aft.

During the time these affairs were going on upon the ship, the southern horizon was lit up again and again by vivid flashes. It appeared to sink into a deeper gloom afterward, but in another moment we heard the distant boom of thunder. Before we could get the topgallantsail set there was a blinding flash off the bow-port, followed by a deep rolling peal of thunder. I was standing in the waist and sprang to Trunnell's room—

"All hands!" I bawled.

Then I rushed for the mizzen rigging, yelling for the men to clew down the t'gallantsail and let the topsail halyards go by the run. At the cry for all hands the men tumbled out, looking around to see what had happened. It was dead still, and the only sounds were the cries of the men on deck to those aloft, and the rattling of gear. Trunnell was on deck in a moment, and as he rushed aft I went for the main rigging with the intention of saving the upper topsail if I could. It was quick work getting up those ratlines, but even as I went I heard a deepening murmur from the southward. The yard came down by the run as I gained the top, owing to Trunnell having cast off everything, trusting that we might get some stops on the sail before too late. I heard the skipper roaring out orders to "hurry there," followed by curses at the slowness of the work. He appeared to realize now what was happening, and it sobered him.

As I crawled out to starboard with a couple of hands, Jackson of Trunnell's watch and Davis of mine, the murmur to the southward swelled rapidly in volume. I glanced into the blackness, and as I did so there was a blinding flash. My eyes seemed to be burned out with the brightness, and a crashing roar thundered in my ears. Instantly afterward I heard Trunnell's voice:—

"Hard up the wheel. Hard up, for God's sake!"

Then, with a rush that made the mast creak with the strain and laid us slowly over amid a thunder of thrashing canvas, the hurricane struck the ship.

There was nothing to do but hold on with both hands and feet. Jackson, who was outside of me, gripped the jackstay and threw his feet around the yard-arm which was springing and jumping away at a terrific rate with the shock of the cracking topsail. I did likewise, and noticed that the canvas was bellying forward, which showed that we were not aback. If we were, I knew our lives were only questions of seconds. All sounds from below were silenced in the roar about us, but flash after flash, following rapidly in succession, showed me momentary glimpses of the deck.

We were far over the water as the *Pirate* was laying down with her topgallant rail beneath the sea. The mizzen topsail had disappeared, as though made of vapor, leaving the mizzen clear. Forward, the two topsails and fore topmast staysail were holding, but between the flashes the upper canvas melted away like a puff of steam, the ragged ends flying and thrashing into long ribbons to leeward. Three men were on the yard when I looked at first, and then, almost instantly afterward, the yard was bare. Whether they had gone overboard I could not tell, but the thought made me look to myself while I might.

Pulling myself along the jackstay until I reached the bunt, I managed to grasp a line that was tailing taut downward toward the deck. This I grasped quickly with both hands, and bawling with all my might to Jackson and Davis to follow, I swung clear of the yard. Looking below, the sea appeared as white as milk in the ghastly light, with the ship's outline now dimly discernible in contrast. I breathed a prayer that the line was fast amidships and slid down.

There was a terrific ripping instantly overhead, and I knew the topsail had gone. The line bowed out with the wind, but led toward the deck near the mast, and in a moment my feet struck the fife rail. I was safe for the present. Jackson followed close upon me, but Davis was unable to get the line. He was never seen again.

Making my way aft by the aid of the weather rail, I reached the poop and climbed up the steps. The wind nearly swept me from my feet, but I managed to crawl aft to where I could make out by the flashes the forms of Trunnell and the skipper.

"She'll go off soon," yelled the mate in my ear. "Nothin' gone forrads yet, hey?"

"Only the canvas and a couple of men," I yelled in reply.

The wind began to draw further and further aft, showing that the ship was gradually gathering headway in spite of her list to starboard. Soon she began to right herself in the storm-torn sea. All was white as snow about us, and the whiteness gave a ghastly light in the gloom. I could now make out the maintopsail, dimly, from where I stood, and the outline of the hull forward. Evidently the fore lower topsail was holding still. Jackson, who was tall and strong, and who was an American by adoption, was put to the lee wheel, as his knowledge of English made him quick to obey. John, a Swede, built very broad with stooping shoulders, and Erikson, a Norwegian with a great blond head and powerful neck, grasped the weather spokes. Bill, the other quartermaster, had not shown up, and we found later that he was one of the missing from the fore topsail yard.

Trunnell and Captain Thompson called the men aft to the poop, and away we went into the gloom ahead.

She was doing a good fifteen knots under her two, or rather one storm topsail; for we found out afterward that the fore had gone almost instantly after she had payed off. The water was roaring white astern, and the wind blew so hard that it was impossible to face it for more than a moment. The sea was making fast, and I began to wonder how long the vessel could run before the great heave which I knew must soon follow us.

Thompson stood bareheaded near the binnacle, and roared to the men to be careful and keep her steady. It was plain he knew nothing of seamanship, but could tell that a thing must be done well after the mate had given orders. He was apparently perfectly sober now, and as cool as though on the beach. It was evident the man feared nothing and could command. I saw that I could be of little use aft, so I started forward, hoping to be able to keep a lookout for a shift of wind and get some gear ready to heave the vessel to.

On reaching the main deck, things showed to be in a hopeless mess. Everything movable had gone to leeward when she was hove down, the running rigging was lying about, and no attempt had been made to coil it. The sea, which had been over the lee rail, had washed that on the starboard side into long tangles which would take hours to clear. I stumbled over a mass of rope which must have been the fore topsail brace. I saw a figure moving through the gloom along the bulwarks and called for the man to lay aft and coil down some of the gear. The man, however, paid no attention to me, but made his way into the forward cabin, and as the door opened and the light from within flashed out I recognized the third mate.

A man named Hans answered my hail, and I started forward again. The sea by this time was running rapidly. The ship was so deep that I knew she would not keep her deck clear, and I started to gain the topgallant forecastle where the height would make it safer.

Just as I gained the highest step, a tremendous sea following broke clear along the top of the rail in the waist, and went forward a good five feet above her bulwarks, the entire length of the main deck.

It was terrific. The thundering crash and smothering jar nearly paralyzed me for a moment. In the dim glare I could see rails, stanchions, boats, rigging, all in the furious white rush. The *Pirate* settled under the load and seemed to stop perfectly still. Then another huge sea went roaring over her and blotted out everything to the edge of the forecastle head.

I stood looking down at the main deck in amazement. How long would the hatches stand that strain? Everything was out of sight under water, save the top of the forward house. I looked up into the roaring void above me and breathed a parting prayer, for it seemed that the ship's end must be at hand. Then I was aware that she was broaching to, and I grabbed the rail to meet the sea.

Every stitch of canvas had gone out of her now, and nothing but the bare yards were left aloft. How they ever stood the frightful strain was a miracle and spoke volumes for the Yankee riggers who fitted her out. The wind bore more and more abeam, and under the pressure she heeled over, letting the great load on her decks roar off in a torrent to leeward, over the topgallant rail and waterways. A sea struck her so heavily that the larger portion of it went thundering clear across her forty feet of deck, landing bodily to leeward as though the ship were below the surface. I could hear a bawling coming faintly from the poop and knew Trunnell was trying to heave her to. Something fluttered from the mizzen rigging and disappeared into the night. Part of a tarpaulin had gone, but it was a chance to get another piece large enough on the ratlines to hold her head up. I tried to make my way aft again to help, for I saw it was about our only hope, and started to crawl along the weather topgallant rail. Then a form sprang from the black recess under the forecastle head and seized me tightly around the body.

VI

The suddenness of this attack and the peculiar position I was in when seized, put me at a disadvantage. The quick breathing of the man behind me, and the strong force he put forward as he rushed me toward the ship's side, made me aware that I was in a bad fix. The assassin was silent as the grave, save for his panting, but his bearded face against mine was visible enough to show me the former captain of the ship.

I was carried half over the rail in an instant by the power of the rush. The foam showed beneath me, and for a moment it seemed that the man would accomplish his deadly purpose. It was with a horrid feeling of certain death before me that I clutched wildly at the forecastle rail. Luckily my hand caught it, and I was saved from the dive over the side. Then with frantic strength I twisted around enough to seize the fellow, and dropped on my knees with a grip around his middle. It was up and down and all over that side of the forecastle head for some minutes, until we were both getting tired. We were apparently alone forward, and the fight would be one of endurance, unless the ruffian happened to have some weapon about him.

We struggled on and on in the gloom, with the hurricane roaring over us, carrying the spray and drift in a smothering storm into our faces. A hand would slip with a wet grip only to take a fresh hold again, and strain away to get the other under.

We rolled with the ship and after a particularly hard rally, in which I had my hand badly bitten, we eased up near the edge of the forecastle head. During this breathing spell I managed to get my foot braced against a ring-bolt. This gave me a slight advantage for a sudden push. In an instant I shoved with all my might, driving us both to the edge. The ruffian saw what was coming and tried to turn, but it was too late. One single instant of frantic fighting, half suspended in the air, and then over we went, myself on top.

We landed heavily upon the main deck, and the shock, falling even as I did upon the body under me, stunned me for several moments. My captain lay motionless. Then, when a sudden rush of cool water poured over us, I came to my senses and started to my feet. In another moment I had passed a line around the desperado, and was dragging him under the lee of the windlass, where I finally made him fast to the bitts.

When I started aft again, I found that Trunnell had managed to get a tarpaulin into the mizzen rigging, and by the aid of this bit of canvas the *Pirate* had at last headed the sea within five points. It now took her forward of the beam and hove her down to her bearings with each roll to leeward, the sea breaking heavily across the main deck, keeping the waterways waist deep with the white surge. In this rush objects showed darkly where they floated from their fastenings until they drifted to a water-port and passed on overboard.

I finally managed to dodge the seas enough to get aft alive, though one caught me under the lee of the fore rigging and nigh smothered me as it poured over the topgallant rail.

Trunnell stood near the break of the poop, and beside him were the skipper and third mate. I noticed a look of surprise come upon the young officer's face when I came close to them. It was much lighter now, and the actions of this young fellow interested me.

"I thought you might have been drowned," he cried, in his high female voice, but with a significant tone and look at the last word which was not lost on me in spite of the elements.

"Everything is all snug forward," I answered, bawling at the captain, but looking fairly at the third mate. "You can let a few men go and rivet irons on the convict by the windlass bitts. He seems to have little trouble unlocking these." And I held up the unlocked irons I had picked up under the forecastle.

As I held the irons under the third officer's nose, he drew back. Then he took them and flung them with an impatient gesture over the side into the sea. I thought I heard a fierce oath in a deep voice near by, but Trunnell and the captain were both staring up at the fringe flying from the maintopsail yard, and had evidently said nothing. There was little more to do now, for as long as the ship held her head to the sea, she would probably ride it out, unless some accident happened.

I was worn out with the exertion from handling canvas and my fracas forward, so after bawling out some of the details of the occurrence into Trunnell's ear, I took my watch below to get a rest. The men who preferred to stay aft clear of the water were allowed to lie down near the mizzen. Some took advantage of this permission, but for the most part they stood huddled in a group along the spanker boom, ready for a call.

I had made it a rule long ago, when I had first gone to sea, that I would never miss a watch below when my turn came if I could be spared with convenience. It is a question always with a sailor when he will be called to shorten sail for a blow, and the best thing he can do is to keep regular hours when he can, and stand by for a crisis when all hands are necessary. With a captain it might be different, for the entire responsibility rests upon him. He also does not have to stand watch, and consequently has no reason to be tired after several hours on deck. But with a sailor or mate who stands his four hours off and on, he must take care he is not pushed beyond his time, for the occasion will certainly come sooner or later when he will have to stand through several watches without a rest. Then, if he is already tired out, he will be useless.

I turned in with a strange feeling about the matter forward and the third officer's conduct. Although I knew Trunnell would take care that the ruffian would not get loose again that night during his watch, I took out a heavy revolver from my locker and stuck it under the pillow of my bunk. Then I saw that the door and port were fast before I jammed myself in for a rest.

I lay a long time thinking over the strange outfit on board, and the more I thought over the matter, the more I became convinced that the third officer had taken a hand in letting Andrews loose to try his hand on me again. There was something uncanny about this officer with a woman's voice, and I actually began to have a secret loathing not entirely unmixed with fear for him.

When I turned out for the morning watch, Trunnell met me in the alleyway. He looked wild and bushy from his exposure to the elements, his hair being in snarls and tangles from having a sou'wester jammed over his ears, and his great flat nose was red from the irritation of the water that struck and streamed over his bearded face. His whiskers gleamed with salt in the light of the lamp, and he spat with great satisfaction as he breathed the quiet air of the cabin.

"It's letting up, Rolling," he said; "there's a little light to the easterd now. Sink me, but we've a job bending gear. Everything gone out of her but her spars, and Lord knows how they stand it. How'd you come to get caught with all that canvas on her?"

"Look here, Trunnell," I answered, "you know I'm a sailor even if I'm not much else, and you know how that canvas came to be on her. I'm almost glad it's gone. I would be if it wasn't for the fact that we'll be longer than usual on this run, and I've about made up my mind that the quicker a decent man gets out of this ship, the better."

I was buttoning up my oilskins while I spoke, and Trunnell smiled a queer bit of a smile, which finally spread over his bearded face and crinkled up the corners of his little eyes into a network of lines and wrinkles. "I heard the outfly," said he, "and I was only joking ye about the canvas. It's a quare world. Ye wouldn't think it, but if ye want to see a true picture of responsibility a-restin' heavy like upon the digestion of a man, ye'll do well to take a good look at the old man a-standin' there on the poop. 'What for?' says you; 'God knows,' says me; but there he is, without a drop o' licker or nothin' in him since he heard ye bellow fer all hands."

"I should think he'd feel a little upset after the way he caught her," I answered; "he probably has the owners' interests a little at heart."

But Trunnell shook his head until the water flew around.

"Ye're off agin, me son. It ain't that at all. That man don't care a whoop for all the owners livin'. Not he. Sink me, Rolling, I got a big head, but nothin' much in it; in spite o' this, though, I knows a thing or two when I sees it. That man has some other object in bein' nervous about this here hooker besides owners. Don't ask me what it is, 'cause I don't know. But I knows what it ain't."

"The whole outfit is queer," I answered, "and the sooner I get out of her, the better satisfied I'll be. No decent sailor would ship in the craft if he could help it."

Trunnell gave me a queer look. Then he saw I meant no offence and shook his great head again.

"Did it ever occur to ye that ye had a duty to do in the world beside huntin' soft jobs?"

"Certainly not that of hunting hard ones," I answered, fastening my belt.

Trunnell's face underwent a change. He was serious and waited until I had strapped my sou'wester under my chin before saying anything.

"Mebbe I'm wrong, an' mebbe I ain't," he said. "But I believes a man has duties to stick to while he's on watch above water. One of these is not to turn tail and scud away, a-showin' your stern to every hard thing as comes along. No, sir, when ye runs into a hard gang like some o' these here aboard this hooker, stick to her, says me. If every man who's honest should turn his stern to a wessel that's got a bad name, what would happen to her? Why, any suckin' swab of a cabin boy kin tell that she'd get worse an' worse with the bad ones what would take your place. Ain't that reason? There's got to be some men to man a ship, an' if no honest ones will, then the owners can't do less than hire raskils. Ye can't sink a ship just because things have happened aboard her. Oh, Lord, no. Think a bit, Rolling, an' tell me if ye ain't blamed glad ye ware here, an' bein' here, ye must 'a' saved some poor devil of a sailor from getting killed this voyage?"

"I'm blamed sorry I ever—"

"Well, now, suppose'n I had a been ashore the day ye had the fracas on the main deck. Where'd ye been now, hey? A hunderd fathom deep, sure as Andrews is aboard this here ship, if I knows anything o' his ways, an' I've sailed two voyages with him afore. No, man; brace up and do yer dooty as ye may. If every good man was to stay out of bad ships, they'd get so the devil himself would be afeard to go to sea in them."

I smiled at the little fellow. Here was a man, who had the reputation of being but little better than an unhung pirate, preaching a most unselfish doctrine. We had been below for several minutes, and I could hear the captain's voice bawling out some order on the deck overhead. The bells were struck by the automatic clock in the cabin, and I turned to go.

"You're a good Christian, anyhow, Trunnell," I said as I started.

Trunnell gave a snort and threw his quid in a corner near a cuspidor. "I ain't never seen the inside of a church. I only tries to do the square thing to whoever is a-runnin' of the sea outfit—same as ye'll do if ye'll take the trouble to think a minit—"

I was out on the deck, and the wind almost blew me into the scuppers. The captain was standing right above me on the poop watching the growing light in the east. The waist was full of foamy water that roared and surged and washed everything movable about. Above, the masts and spars looked dark in the dim, gray light of the early morning, the strips of canvas stretching away from the jackstays and flicking dismally to leeward. All the yards, however, were trimmed nicely, showing Trunnell's master hand, and on the mainmast, bellying and straining with the pressure, was a new storm spencer, set snug and true, holding the plunging vessel up to the great rolling sea that came like a living hill from the southwest. Forward, a bit of a staysail was set as taut as a drumhead, looking no bigger than a good-sized handkerchief. Aft, a trysail, set on the spanker boom, helped the tarpaulin in the mizzen to bring her head to the sea.

I climbed up the poop ladder and took a look around.

It was a dismal sight. As far as the eye could reach through the white haze of the flying drift the ocean presented a dirty steel-gray color, torn into long, ragged streaks of white where the combers rolled on the high seas before the gale. Overhead all was a deep blank of gray vapor. The wind was not blowing nearly as hard as it had during my last watch on deck, but the sea was rolling heavier. It took the *Pirate* fair on the port bow, and every now and again it rose so high above her topgallant rail that it showed green light through the mass that would crash over to the deck and go roaring white to leeward, making the main deck uninhabitable. Sometimes a heavy, quick comber would strike her on the bluff of the bow, and the shock would almost knock the men off their feet. Then the burst of water would shoot high in the air, going sometimes clear to the topgallant yard, nearly a hundred feet above the deck, while all forward would disappear in the flying spray and spume.

"Fine weather, Rolling, hey?" bawled the skipper to me as I gained the poop.

"Oh, it isn't so bad the way she's taking it now. If she hangs on as well as this during the watch, she'll make good weather of it all right," I said.

"I'm glad you think so, my son. Just call down to the steward to bring me a bracer. Whew, just look at that!"

As he spoke a huge sea rose on the weather bow and bore down on the staggering ship. It struck her fair and rolled over her so heavily that I had to grab a line to keep from being knocked down. The main deck was full of water, and as it roared off through the ports and over the lee rail, I looked to see if anything had gone with it. Then I realized how well we had been washed during the night.

From the forecastle aft to the poop there was nothing left except the hatches and deck-house. The boats were all stove to matchwood except one that was lashed on the forward house. The bulwarks were smashed for many feet along both sides, but this was no real damage, as it allowed the sea to run off easier, relieving the deck of the heavy load. The whole main deck, fore and aft, was as clean stripped as could be, and the hatches alone were saving us from filling and going under.

It was a dismal sight, and the men who stood huddled on the forecastle and poop looked, in their yellow oilskins, like so many yellow ghosts. I went aft to the wheel and found that Hans and Johnson were steering without much difficulty, although they had all they could do to hold her when a sea struck aft. Far astern the light seemed to be growing brighter, and while I looked there appeared some long streaks in the heavy banks of vapor which showed a break or two. I took the glass which hung on the side of the grating and cleaned the lens with my hand. Sweeping the storm-torn horizon to the southward, nothing showed but rolling seas and haze. I turned the glass to the northward, and in a moment I saw a black speck rise and then disappear from the line of vision.

"Vessel to lor'ard, sir," I bawled to the captain.

"I don't care for forty vessels, Rolling. Get me that steward with the liquor, or there'll be one afloat here without a second mate."

VII

It was with no good feeling that I went below to get the old man a drink. The steward met me and grinned as he brought forth the liquor.

"Yessah, it's nine ob dem he takes endurin' de watch. Lord, man, he's got something pow'rful on his mind. Did yo' ebber feel the heft ob his trunk he brought aboard, sah? No, sah, dat yo' didn't. Well, it's pow'rful heavy fo' a man's baggage."

"What's in it?" I asked.

"'Deed, I doan know, man, jest what is in it, but I reckon it's something what worries him. Dat an' Cap'n Andrews forrads worries him some. Chips, he say as dey goes aft an' have matters straightened out a bit. Dey is fo' either weldin' irons on de cap'n forrads or puttin' him on de beach. Jim, Hans, Bendin, an' Frenchy an' a lot more are fo' doing' somethin' with him. Yessah, dey is dat. Hab a leetle nip 'fore yo' goes?"

I took one and went back to the quarter-deck. The speck to leeward showed a bit of storm canvas flying, and we soon could make out she was a large ship hove to like ourselves on the port tack. Her hull showed now and again on the seas, and after drifting down toward her for about an hour, the light grew strong enough to make her out plainly. She was a large ship, English built, with a turtle-backed stern, painted white on the tumble-home of the quarter. Her hull was black, and the foam showed in long white lines of streamers as it was blown across her topsides. She was making heavy weather of it, and every now and again she would ram her nose clear out of sight in the high-rolling sea. Then she would rise heavily, with the white water pouring from her dripping forefoot and wallow dismally, until her weather rail would appear to roll under.

The stump of a foremast showed forward and a stout maintopsail strained away amidships, while aft, where the mizzen should have been, there was nothing showing above her deck. Her main topgallant mast was also gone at the cross-trees, but the maintopsail held strongly. Altogether she was pretty well wrecked aloft.

While we watched her we drew nearer, and when she came within a couple of miles I could make out a flag, the English ensign, union down, in the main rigging. This showed pretty plainly that she was doing badly and wanted help, but it was absolutely useless to think of doing anything for her while the wind held and the sea showed no signs of going down.

Being much lighter than she was, we drifted off more, and we came nearer and nearer as the morning brightened into a dirty day. In a short time we had her close under our lee, not half a mile distant. Indeed, it looked as though we might get closer than we wished to. The wind slacked gradually, however, and before long we managed to get out our main-topmast staysail. Then followed a close-reefed foresail balanced aft by the mizzen lower topsail, which we had saved. This, with the spencer and canvas already set, gave us a good hold of the ship in spite of the sea, and we were ready to wear if necessary. The *Pirate* drifted much faster under the extra canvas and went to leeward so far that we saw that she would go clear of the stranger. As we drew near, we now saw how deep she sat in the water, the seas rolling over her, amidships, with every plunge. Still she headed up well and was under control.

While we gazed, a string of flags fluttered from her yard-arm. I dived below for the code and soon read the signal for help. They were sinking.

Trunnell turned out on deck, and we waited to see if Captain Thompson would give the word to do anything. He stood near the rail and gazed through his glass without saying anything or exhibiting any concern whatever for the people we could now see upon the stranger's high poop.

Then he turned to the mate and asked:—

"What does he want, Trunnell?"

"Want's us to stand by him, I reckon," the mate replied.

"Can we do it without danger in this seaway, hey?" demanded Thompson. "Answer me that. How the devil can we do anything for a fellow in this seaway, when we might be rammed by him and sink ourselves?"

"We'll stand by that ship as long as she's above water," answered Trunnell, quietly.

Then came a sudden change upon the captain. He turned upon the mate quickly, and his bright, glinting eyes seemed to grow to sharp points on either side of his hooked nose, which worked and twitched under the excitement. His hand went behind his back and he jerked forth a long revolver.

"Who's captain of this here boat, Mr. Trunnell, me or you?" said he, in his drawling voice.

"You," answered Trunnell, decisively.

"Do you presume to give any orders here what don't agree with mine?"

"No, sir," said Trunnell.

"Well, just let me hint to you, you bushy-headed little brute, that I don't want any suggestions from my mates, see? You little snipe, you! what d'ye mean, anyhow, by saying what we'll do?"

Several men standing on the poop to keep clear of the seas in the waist, hitched their trousers a little, and felt for the sheath knives in their belts. I noticed Jim, the young landsman, pass his hand behind him and stand waiting. There was an ominous silence and watchfulness among the crew which was not lost on the captain. He had inspired no respect in their minds as a sailor, even though he had shown himself fearless. It was evident that they were with Trunnell.

"I meant that we would stand by that ship as long as she floated," said the little mate, looking straight into the pistol barrel, "and I expected that it would be by your orders, sir."

Thompson was not a fool. He saw in an instant how the case was, and his glinting eyes took in the whole outfit of men and mates at one glance. He may not have wished to help the strangers, but he saw that not to do so meant more trouble to himself than if he did.

"This time you expected just right, Trunnell. I mean to stand by those people, and I order you to get ropes ready to hoist out the boat we have on the house, there. What I don't want and won't have is orders suggested by any one aboard here but me. I'm glad you didn't mean to do that, for I'd hate to kill you. You can get the boat ready."

Then he put the revolver back into his pocket, and Trunnell went forward along the shelter of the weather bulwarks and made ready the tackles for hoisting the boat out.

By the aid of the powerful glass I made out a figure of a woman standing upon the ship's poop. She appeared to be watching us intently. Soon a little sailorly and seaman-like fellow named Ford, whose interest in the strange ship was marked, came from the group near the mizzen and asked if he should get the signal halyards ready. Thompson made no objection, and we bent on the flags which told by the code that we would stand by them until the sea went down enough to get out a small boat.

At seven bells the "doctor" managed to get some fire started in the galley, and all hands had a drink of hot coffee. This was cheering, and Trunnell soon had the watch hard at work getting out new canvas from the lazaretto aft. The main deck was getting safer, and although she took the sea heavily now and then, she was no longer like a half-tide rock in a strong current.

Topsails were hoisted out from below and gantlines bent. By the time all hands had eaten something and eight bells had struck, we were ready to get up new topsails and start the pumps.

Luckily there was little water below. In spite of the tremendous straining the ship had made no more than could be expected, and in a little over an hour at the brakes we had the satisfaction of having the pumps suck.

All that morning we worked aloft getting new gear up. The British ship drew away on our weather beam, wallowing horribly in the seaway. The wind died away gradually into a good stiff gale, and by noon we had a break or two above us that let down the sunlight. This cheered all hands. A good meal with extra coffee was served forward, and I sat down to the cabin table with Chips and the steward, to eat ravenously of prime junk and preserved potatoes.

"'Tis a quare time ye had ag'in last night, forrads, hey?" said Chips.

"It was interesting for a few minutes," I answered. "I hope you fixed the fellow's irons all right. Keys seem to have strange ways aboard this vessel."

"Well, ye needn't be afear'd av th' raskil takin' leave ag'in. Sure, an' I riveted his irons this time, as will take a file an' no less to cut through. I votes we get th' old man to put him aboard th' first ship what comes a-heavin' down nigh enough, hey?"

"It would suit me all right," I answered.

"Jim and Long Tom an' Hans an' a whole lot av us have th' matter in mind, an' we'll speak wid th' skipper afore long. There's a divil's mess below in th' fore-peak, where a barrel has bruk loose that I'll have to mix wid first. Be ye a-goin' in th' boat aboard th' stranger whin th' sea goes down?"

"I suppose so," I said; "that lot generally falls to a second mate."

"Be sure, thin, ye have th' plug in all right an' th' oars sound, fer th' sea will be heavy fer a bad craft, and ye mind th' irons last night."

"I'll just take a look at them before I start. Chips," I said. "Thank you for keeping tabs on the skipper."

"It's no great matter," he answered; and then we fell to with a will until the meal was finished.

VIII

At three bells in the afternoon the sea had begun to go down enough to allow us to get our new topsails on her and a main-topgallantsail. The *Pirate* went smoking through it under the pressure, trembling with each surge, and throwing a perfect storm of water over her catheads. The English ship was now a mere speck to windward, almost hull down, and we would have to beat up to her if we could.

Just how badly she needed help we of course could not tell. If she were sinking fast, then she would have to depend upon her own boats, for the sea was too heavy until late in the afternoon to venture out in our only one left. We could no longer see her signals, but carried all the sail possible, without danger of carrying away our spars, in the effort to get close to her again.

After standing along for an hour or more we wore ship, and found that we could just about get within hailing distance to leeward.

Trunnell had the reef tackles rigged from the main yard, and the life-boat was slung clear of the lee rail. Then, watching a chance, she was let go with Hans and Johnson in her to keep her clear and dropped back to the mizzen channels, where the volunteers were ready to get aboard her.

Four men besides myself manned her, and she was instantly let go to keep her clear of the sea, which hove her first high on the *Pirate's* quarter, and then down until our faces were below the copper on her bends. By dint of quick work we shoved her clear, and started on the pull, dead to windward.

How small the *Pirate* looked when we were but a few fathoms distant in that sea! Our boat rode the waves nicely without shipping much water, and several times I turned to look back at the ship, where Trunnell stood beside the skipper, watching us through the glasses, and waiting to pick us up on our return. I could see the "doctor's" face above the topgallant rail forward and that of Chips in the waist.

It was a long pull. The sea was running high and the wind was still blowing a half gale, breaking up the heavy oily clouds into long banks between which the sun shone at intervals. It was a good half hour's work before we could cover the short distance between the ships.

We came slowly up under her lee quarter, and when we were quite close I could see that she was indeed very deep, if not actually sinking. The words "Royal Sovereign, Liverpool," were painted in gold letters on her stern, and on the circular buoys hanging upon her quarter-rail was the same name in black. A group of men stood near the mizzen rigging, and one short man with a black sou'wester and blue pilot coat hailed us through a large-mouthed trumpet, which almost hid his bearded face.

"Boat ahoy! can you come aboard?" he roared.

"We'll try to come alongside," I bawled. "Stand by to heave a line."

A man had one ready and hove it well out with a yell to catch. Long Tom, our lean Yankee sailor, who was pulling bow oar, seized it as it fell across and took a turn around a thwart. The oars were shipped and we fell under the vessel's stern, riding the seas without mishap.

"We're sinking," cried the short man, who was the captain. "Can you take some of us with you?"

"Aye, aye; get them aboard here as quick as you can," came the answer.

There was no time lost now. Men swarmed toward the taffrail, and for an instant it looked as if there would be something of a panic. The short skipper, however, flung them aside without ceremony, and the next instant a female figure appeared at the rail.

"Haul easy," came the order. Hans and Tom pulled in the line slowly until the boat's bow was leading almost directly beneath the ship's stern. A bridle was rigged from the spanker boom and made fast to a life buoy. Then the lady who had appeared at the taffrail was slung in it rather uncomfortably and carefully lowered away. She was seized by one of the men forward, and handed aft to me.

The woman was quite young. She was slightly built, and I supported her easily until she was safely in the stern sheets. A few strands of curly blond hair blew across my face, and gave me a most peculiar feeling as I brushed them aside. Then she turned up her face, and I saw that she had most beautiful eyes, soft and gentle, with a trusting look, such as one sees in children.

"Thank you, Mr. Sailorman," she said, with a smile. "I'm all right now."

"Except, perhaps, for a little wetting, you will stay so, I hope," I answered.

A heavy woman was being lowered away, and Hans caught her boldly around the body, trying to keep her from being thrown out of the tossing small boat. She shrieked dismally.

"Don't be silly, mamma," cried the young lady aft. "You've been squeezed tighter than that before, I am sure."

She was passed aft and took her place beside her daughter in the stern, expostulating incoherently at the younger one's insinuations.

Then followed a little man, short and stout, who was evidently the ship's carpenter, and he was followed by a dozen sailors.

"Haven't you any boats that will swim?" I asked of the mate, who hung over the rail above me.

"We're getting them out now," he answered.

"Then let us go. We've got a big enough load already."

In a few moments we were on our way back to the *Pirate*, making good headway before the wind and sea, and shipping little water.

The men explained as we went along that the *Sovereign* had started a butt during the gale, and she was full of water by this time. They had kept at the pumps all day, but had given it up when they saw we were coming for them. The ship's cargo of oil and light woods from the peninsula had kept her from going to the bottom. She was homeward bound to Liverpool, and it was the captain's wife and daughter we were bringing aboard. The hurricane had caught them aback and dismasted them during the night, and after six hours of plunging helplessly into the sea without anything but the mainmast and stump of the foremast above the deck, she had sprung a leak and filled rapidly. The maintopsail they had bent in the morning after extraordinary exertion, and with this they had managed to keep her partly under control.

"She will never go to the bottom with all the soft wood she has in her," said a sailor who was old and grizzled and had the bearing of a man-of-war's man. "She can't sink for months. The water is up to her lower deck already."

"So that's the reason you were not getting your boats out in a hurry?" I asked.

"Sure," said he; "I'd as soon stay in her a bit longer as in many a bleedin' craft that you sees a-goin' in this trade."

"I noticed you were one of the first to leave her," said the young girl, with some spirit.

"Ah, mum, when you gets along in life like me, hardships is not good for the constitootion. A sailorman, 'e gets enough o' them without huntin' any more. Howsumever, if I see any chance o' gettin' the bleedin' craft in port 'way out here in this Hindian Ocean, I'd be the last to leave. Bust me, mum, if that ain't the whole truth, an' a little more besides. You ask your pa."

Here he gave a sigh, and drew his hand across his forehead as if in pain. His large pop eyes blinked sadly for a few moments, and his mouth dropped down at the corners. Then his mahogany-colored face became fixed and his gaze was upon the craft he had just deserted. What was in the old fellow's mind? I really felt sorry for him, as he sat there gazing sadly after his deserted home. Captain Sackett would stay aboard until the last, his wife informed us, but as there was no necessity of any one staying now, if their boats could live in the sea that was still running, it was probable that they would all be aboard us before night. Jenks, the old sailor, gave it as his opinion that they would have the boats out in half an hour.

We came up under the lee of the *Pirate* and then began the job of getting our passengers aboard her.

Trunnell passed a line over the main-brace bumpkin, and held the tossing craft away from the ship's side until a bridle could be bent and the ladies hoisted aboard.

Mrs. Sackett trembled violently and begged that she would not be killed, much to her daughter's amusement. Finally she was landed on deck, where she was greeted by the third mate and escorted aft. Miss Sackett was of different stuff. She insisted that she could grab the mizzen channel plates and climb aboard. I begged her to desist and be hoisted on deck properly, but she gave me such a look that I held back and refrained from passing the line about her. As the boat lifted on a sea she made a spring for the channel. Her hand caught it all right, but her foot slipped, and as the boat sank into the hollow trough she was left hanging.

Trunnell instantly sprang over the side, and letting himself down upon the channel, seized her hand and lifted her easily to a footing. The ship rolled down until they were knee deep in the sea, but the little mate held tight, and then, with one hand above his head, as she rose again, he lifted his burden easily to the grasp of Jim, who reached over the side for her.

After she was landed safely the men crowded up the best way they could, and the boat was dropped astern with a long painter to keep her clear of the ship's side.

Captain Thompson greeted his female passengers awkwardly. He declared in a drawling tone that he was 'most glad that their boat was wrecked, inasmuch as it had given him the opportunity to meet the finest ladies he had ever set eyes on.

"May the devil grasp me in his holy embrace, madam," said he, "if I am lying when I says that word. It is my most pious thought, says I."

Mrs. Sackett was somewhat taken aback at this candor, but managed to keep her feelings well hidden. Her daughter came to the rescue. "We appreciate your noble efforts, Captain Thompson. The fact is, we have heard so much about your gallantry in saving life at sea that we are sure anything we could say would sound weak in comparison to what you must already have heard. If you have a spare stateroom, we would be very thankful if we might have it for a time, as our clothes are quite wet from the sea."

The skipper was somewhat surprised at the young girl's answer, but he hid his confusion by bawling for the steward.

When the mulatto came, he gave numerous orders in regard to bunks, linen, drying of clothes, etc., regretting over and over again that he was a single man, and consequently had no wife from whom he could borrow wearing apparel while that of his guests was drying.

The third mate, also, took pains to be very civil to them, and his soft voice could be heard in conversation with Miss Sackett long after they had gone below.

I went forward and interviewed the men we had rescued, afterward getting the "doctor" to serve them something hot, as their galley fire had been out many hours and they had been eating nothing but ship's bread.

The *Pirate* waited all the afternoon with her canvas shortened down to her lower topsails to keep her from forging ahead too fast. But even when it grew dark and the British ship could no longer be clearly made out, her skipper had not gotten out his boats. It was evident that he would try to save her if possible, and now that his family were safe he cared little for the risk. Captain Thompson still held the *Pirate* hove to under easy canvas, drifting slowly with the wind, which was now no more than a moderate breeze. The sea, also, was going down fast, and the sky was showing well between the long lines of greasy-looking clouds which appeared to sail slowly away to the northeast. The night fell with every prospect of good weather coming on the following day.

I went on deck in the dog-watch and took a look around. The *Sovereign* was a mere blur on the horizon, but her lights shone clearly.

"We'll stand by her all night," said Trunnell, "and then if the skipper doesn't care to leave her,—which he will, however,—we'll stand away again."

There was little to do, so the watch lounged around the deck and rested from the exertion of the past twenty-four hours. Chips told me I had better come forward after supper and take a smoke in his room, for they were going to come to some conclusion about the fellow Andrews. There had been some talk of putting him aboard the English ship, and if we could get the captain to agree to it, it would be done.

I loafed around until I saw a light between the crack of his door and the bulkhead. Then I slid it back, and entered.

The stuffy little box was full of men. The bos'n, a large man named Spurgen, who had quite a swagger for a merchant sailor, was holding forth to the quartermaster, Hans, on nautical operations.

"An' how'd ye do if ye had an anchor atween, decks widout nothin' to hoist it out wid?" he was saying as I came in.

Hans affirmed, with many oaths, that he'd let the "bloody hancor go bloomin' well to the bottom before he'd fool wid it." This made the bos'n angry, and he opened with a fierce harangue, accompanied by a description of the necessary manoeuvres. He also made some remarks relating to the quartermaster's knowledge of things nautical.

I took occasion to look about the little room while this was going on and my fingers warmed up some. I then seated myself on a corner of the chest near Chips to make myself easy, during which time the bos'n had gained sufficient ground to enforce silence upon his adversary, and relinquish the subject of anchors. Then came a pause during which I could distinguish the "doctor's" voice above the mutterings, and get a whiff of my own tobacco out of the haze.

"—five fat roaches; they'll cure you every time," he was saying to Chips. "It's old man Green's sure remedy, sah, yes, sah. I hearn him tole his ole mate, Mr. Gantline, when he sailed in the West Coast trade."

"Faith, ye may stave me, shipmate, but that would be an all-fired tough dish to swallow," the carpenter declared, with a wry face. "Supposen they didn't die? They would make a most eternal disagreeable cargo shiftin' about amongst your ribs. May the devil grab me, ye moke, if I wouldn't rather swell up an' bust wid th' scurvy than swallow them fellows kickin'."

"Bile 'em, white man," said the cook. "Bile 'em in er pint er water—an' then fling 'em overboard. Who the debble would eat er roach?"

"Right ye are, shipmate," assented Chips; "'tis an aisy enough dose to take if all ye do is to throw th' critters to lor'ard. Sink me, though, if I sees th' benefit av a medicine ye fling to David Jones instead av placin' it to th' credit av yer own innerds."

"Yah, yah, Mr. Chips, but you beats me. Yes, sah, you beats me, but yer haid is thick. Yes, sah, yer haid is thick ernuff, yah, yah," laughed the "doctor." "What would yer do but drink the water, white man? yes, sah, drink the water for the acid in the critter. It's salt in yer blood makes scurvy, from libbin' so long er eatin' nuffin' but salt junk. Lime juice is good, ef the ole man gives it to yer straight, but he nebber does. No, sah, dat he nebber do. It's too expensive. Anyways, it doan' hab no strength like er roach, ner no sech freshness, which am de main pint after all."

Seeing himself out of the talk, and having completely growled down the quartermaster, the bos'n started another subject. This was a tirade against bad skippers and crimps who stood in too thick with the shipping commissioners, and whom he swore were in league with each other and the devil. He was an old sailor, and his seamed face was expressive when launching into a favorite subject. Here was Jim's chance, and he spoke out. "Whatever became of Jameson, what was took off by Andrews?" he asked Chipps.

"Was he doped?" I asked.

"Didn't ye niver hear tell from O'Toole an' Garnett? They was Andrews's mates for a spell, until th' Irishman, God bless him, knocked him overboards an' nearly killed him in a scuffle on th' India Docks."

"Cast loose; I want to hear," said the bos'n.

There was a moment's silence, and Chips looked at me as though questioning the senior officer of his watch. Then he fixed himself comfortably on the chest by jamming himself against the bulkhead, locking his hands about his knees, blowing smoke in a thick cloud.

I heard the hail of Trunnell from the bridge during this pause, asking about a t'gallant leach-line. Thinking it well to take a look out, I did so to see if the men obeyed his orders, and found them rather slow slacking the line. This made it necessary for me to take a hand in matters and instil a little discipline among them, which kept me on deck for some minutes.

IX

When I had a chance to slip back into the forward house, Chips had already "cast loose" and was in full swing.

"There ain't no use of tellin' everything one sees aboard ship," he was saying, "for you know whin things happen on deep water th' world ain't much th' wiser fer hearing about them. There ain't no telegraphs, an' th' only witnesses is the men concerned—or the wimmen. The men may or mayn't say a thing or two after getting the run av th' beach, but as th' critters have to wait half a year afore getting there, the news av th' occurrence wears off an' regard for the effects on th' teller takes place. It's just as often as not th' men keep mum. You know that as well as I do.

"This same Andrews as is forrads in irons was running the *Starbuck* with Jameson as mate, an' old Garnett as second under him. Ye all know that old pirit. But this time he didn't have any hand in Andrews's game. Andrews wanted to marry the girl Jameson had, an' whin he found he had lost her he played his devil's trick.

"Jameson hadn't been married a week afore Andrews took him around b' th' foot av Powell Street in 'Frisco an' set up some drinks. That's the last any one sees av Jameson fer a year or more on th' West Coast, fer whin he comes to, he was at sea on that old tank, th' *Baldwin*, an' old man Jacobs would as soon have landed him on th'moon as put him ashore."

"A purty bloomin' mean trick," interrupted the bos'n.

"Th' poor divil did have a hard time av it, fer he wasn't a very fierce sort o' chap. He ware a gentil spoken, kind-hearted feller, an' ye know well enough how a man what isn't made of iron wud git along wid Jacobs or his mates. They hazed him terrible; an', as they ware one hundred an' seventy days an' nights to Liverpool, he took the scurvy. Ye can reckon what was left av him afterwards. Whin he left th' hospital, he was glad enough to ship on a Chilean liner to get even as far to the West Coast as Valparaiso.

"He ware aboard this Dago, puttin' in, whin he saw th' *Starbuck* standin' out o' th' harbor. His wife ware on th' quarter-deck—"

"That's the way with most women," snarled the bos'n, interrupting.

"I don't know about that," continued Chips. "You see, after he had been gone a few months, an' Andrews had been hangin' around all th' time gettin' in his pisonous work, she began to have a little faith in th' villain. It wasn't long afore he convinced her Jameson had deserted, fer he proved fair enough he had shipped aboard th' *Baldwin*, without so much as saying good-by. There ware plenty of men to back him on that, includin' th' boatman what rowed them aboard. Finally, partly by blandanderin' an' a-feelin' around, fer th' poor gal ware now alone in th' world, he got her to step aboard th' bleedin' hooker *Starbuck* the day he ware ready for sea. Thin he jest stood out—an'—an'—well, after they'd been out six months th' matter ended as far as Jameson ware concerned.

"Jameson took the news hard whin he got th' run av th' beach, but he was that kindly disposed chap an' went along th' best he could until th' war broke out. He ware still waitin' at Valparaiso whin they drafted him into the Dago army, an' he was lucky enough to be on th' side what got licked. Then there ware no use waitin' there fer th' *Starbuck* to come in again, so he made a slant for Peru as they niver took no pris'ners. Two weeks afterwards Andrews came in again fer nitrates wid Garnett an' O'Toole fer mates—"

"Lucky fer Andrews he wasn't there," said the bos'n; "he'd have had his ornery hide shot full of holes."

"What's th' use av ye talking like a fool?" said Chips. "Is shootin' up a feller a-goin' to undo a wrong like that? Th' shootin' was all done on th' other side, an' Andrews is sound yet an' aboard this here ship. Some men think av other things besides revenge. Especially kind-hearted fellers like Jameson what niver cud hurt no one. As soon as some av Jameson's friends who knew of th' affair told his wife, she wint right into th' cabin where Andrews was, an' afore he knew what she ware up to, she had shot herself. Andrews paid her funeral expenses, an' buried her in th' little Dago cemetery out forninst th' city gate. An' thin Garnett, who didn't know av his skipper's diviltry, sware vengeance on th' husband who deserted her, fer she ware gentil and kind wid th' men forrads."

Here Chips paused and gave me a sidelong look as he refilled his pipe. Then he lit it and smiled hopefully.

"They ware a quare pair, them mates, Garnett an' O'Toole," he said. "What one wasn't th' other was, and *wice wersa*. They lay there two months loadin' on account o' th' war having blocked th' nitrate beds.

"Wan day O'Toole saw an old woman come limpin' along th' dock where th' *Starbuck* lay. She hobbled on to th' gang-plank an' started aboard, an' O'Toole began to chaff Garnett. He waren't half bad as a joker.

""Pon me whurd, Garnett,' sez he, 'I do belave your own mother is comin' aboard to visit ye—but no, maybe it's yer swatheart, fer ye have an uncommon quare taste, ye know. B' th' saints, ye ware always a bold one fer th' ladies.'

"We ware lying in th' next berth, not twenty feet away, an' from where I sat on th' rail I cud hear thim talk an' see what was a-goin' on.

"'Stave me,' says old Garnett, solemn like, 'that's true enough. Sink her fer a fool, though, to be a-comin' down here to win back an old windjammer like me—What? ye mean that old hag driftin' along the deck? Blast you for a red-headed shell-back, d'ye s'pose I'd take up wid wimmen av your choice? No, I never makes a superior officer jealous;' an' wid that he takes out his rag an' mops th' dent in th' top av his head where there's no hair nor nothin' but grease, an' he draws out his little pestiverous vial av peppermint salts an' sniffs.

"'Faith, an' ye'll need to clear yer old head, ye owld raskil, ye've been too gay fer onct,' says O'Toole.

"She ware a tough-lookin' old gal, an' her hat brim flopped over her face. O'Toole met her an' pointed to Garnett.

"'If it's th' leddy-killer av th' fleet ye're afther, there he Stan's.'

"Th' old woman looked an' stopped.

"'No,' says she, in a sort o' jangled tone, 'eets my little gal I looks fer—she's aboard here wid th' capt'in,'

"'Ye can't see her,' says Garnett, 'an' ye better get ashore afore I calls one av thim Dago soldiers to carry ye off an' marry ye.'

"I cud jest get th' glint av th' old woman's eyes, then she bent her head lower.

"'E—eets my leetle gal I must see,' an' there was somethin' in her voice that made one pay attention, 'twas so deep an' solemn like. I ware listening an' a few soldiers av th' army what was camped in th' town came up an' stopped an' looked on.

"'She ware a good leetle gal—an' I cared for her—Yes, by God, she ware a good gal,' said th' old one, hoarsely.

"I cud see O'Toole turn away his head an' Garnett sniff hard at his vial. 'Twas good, he used to say, fer things in th' head. Thin he turned to th' old woman.

"'Ye better get ashore, old gal, she ain't aboard here. We don't take thim kind on deep water.'

"'I must see her afore I goes,' says th' old woman, an' her voice ware a whisper that died away, but ware so full av force O'Toole turned to her.

"'Was it Mrs. Jameson ye wished to see?' he asked.

"The old woman nodded.

"'Well—er—faith, an' she—er,' an' thin he stopped to look at Garnett.

"'She had an accident, by yer lave, 'bout a month ago. How was it ye niver hearn tell? Waren't ye here whin th' old man brought her ashore?'

"'I come from 'Frisco,' says she.

"'Well, I s'pose ye might as well know now as niver,' O'Toole blurted out; 'she's dead, owld woman. Been dead a month gone. Th' old man buried her dacent like, fer, as ye say, she ware a rale good gal, 'pon me whurd, fer a fact, she ware that. 'Tis hard to tell ye, but it's th' truth, th' whole truth, an' divil a bit besides.'

"While he talked th' old woman's head went lower, and whin he finished, she gave a hard gasp. Thin she stood huddled forninst th' deck-house, an' Garnett started forward to th' men at work stevin' th' last av th' cargo.

"All av a sudden like I saw her raise her face an' spit a button from her mouth. Her eyes ware starin' an' lookin' at th' hill away off t' th' eastward av th' town an' beyant to th' great southern mountings av th' Andes range. Thin she slowly straightened up an' walked wid a firm step along th' deck an' th' gang-plank.

"Th' soldier men made way for her on th' dock, but she looked straight beyant her nose an' held her way firm an' strong until she went out av sight, lavin' O'Toole starin' after her.

""Pon me whurd, Garnett,' he called, "tis a most wonderful thing, look!'

""Tis a mother's love, ye haythen; 'pon me whurd, there's nothin' else like it. See how th' news affected th' poor old crayther. It puts me in mind av the time whin I had an old leddy t' look after me. 'Tis a rale jewil av a thing, an' a man only has it th' onct.'

"'More's th' pity,' says Garnett. 'Sink ye, but ye sure are a tough one to tell th' old gal on so short notice. But ye niver did have no feelin's, ye bloomin' heathen.'

""Pon me sowl, what cud I do else?'

"'O' course, 'tain't likely a rough feller like you could do any better, but whin any wimmen folks come aboard agin, come to a man as is used to thim. A man as can talk an' act in a way they likes. A man wid some ways to him. A man—' Here he stooped an' picked up th' button th' old gal had dropped.

"'Where did this come from?' he asked.

"'She had it in her mouth,' says O'Toole.

"'Well, it's one av th' buttons off a uniform that ain't healthy to be wearin' around these parts just now.' An' then they both looked hard at th' little thing.

"'D'ye s'pose it cud have been?' asked O'Toole.

"'Been what?' says Garnett.

"'Jameson, ye blatherin' ijiot. Jameson, th' same as left his wife, a-comin' here huntin' for her. 'Twas so, fer a fact. He had it in his mouth to kape us from knowin' his voice, an' by th' same tokin, I calls to mind th' chokin' in his throat, the scand'lous owld woman he was.'

"'Stave me, but ye might have been right for onct in yer life, so bear a hand an' let's stand away after him an' ketch th' old leddy an' see,' says Garnett.

"They started off without listenin' to my hail, so I climbed down to th' dock an' follows. It was evenin' now, an' th' street was crowded, but they pushed along ahead av me.

"Ye see it ware Jameson, sure enough, an whin he heard his wife ware dead, he wint up that street like a man in a dream. He forgot all about his dress, an' his face ware hard set like a man thinkin' over th' past. He had some five minutes' start av th' mates, an' whin a poor beggar woman spoke to him he scared her half to death with his voice when he asked her th' way to th' cemetery. Thin he remembered his disguise, stepped into a doorway, pulled off th' dress an' hat an' flung thim to th' old beggar woman, an' went his way.

"Garnett an' O'Toole came along a few minutes later an' saw th' beggar.

"'There he is. That's him,' sung out the old sailor, pintin' to th' old gal walkin' along wid her rags tied in a bundle tucked under her arm, fer she had made shift to change thim fer Jameson's slops.

"''Pon me whurd, ye're right fer onct agin,' says O'Toole.

"'Well, don't go a-spoilin' th' thing this time. Let me sail inter him, an' if I wants yer, I'll sing out, an' ye can bear a hand an' help.' Garnett swung across th' street to overhaul th' old woman, an' came up behind her.

"'Evenin', old lady, I wants to have a talk wid ye;' an' he lays his hand on her shoulder wid a grip to take a piece av flesh out. She stopped an' turned quick.

"'*Caramba!*' she yells; 'I teach ye to insult a dacent old lady, you Yankee dog. Help! Murder! ye bloody raskil! Help, help!' Thin she ware upon him like a wild cat, a clawin' an' bitin', screechin' and yellin'.

"'Sink you for a bloody scoundrel, Jameson, I knows ye,' roared Garnett. 'Larry, there, bear a hand. I have him.'

"'Hold him thin, ye brave man,' sings out O'Toole, comin' up. 'Go it, owld gal, give it to him. 'Tis a leddy-killer he is fer sure, 'pon me whurd, fer a fact. Claw him, bite him, even though he's as tough as nails. Yell him deaf, owld leddy. Do it fer his mether's sake, th' scand'lous owld rake he is. Get his year in yer teeth an' hold on, fer 'tis a leddy-killer ye have in yer hands at last. Whang his hide off! Whang him! Whang him!' An' I thought th' old raskil would die av laffin'.

"We ware crowdin' around thim to see th' fun, an' th' way that old gal whanged an' lammed, an' lammed an' whanged, wud have brung tears to yer eyes. 'Twas too much fer human natur' to stan', an' so away goes Garnett down th' street as fast as his bow-legs can git him over th' beach, wid his sheets slacked off a-runnin' free, an' likewise, b' th' same tokin, away squares th' old leddy wid her skysails set an' everythin' drawin' 'cept her skirts, which she holds b' th' clews an' bunts.

"'After him! Catch th' blackguard!' bawls O'Toole, rolling on th' pavement, laffin' an' bawlin'.

"That old beggar was clipper built, fer sure, for wid her skirts clewed up she ware bearin' down fast on th' old mate an' kept his bow-legs a-lurchin' afore th' crowd a-comin' along in th' wake a-yellin' an' hootin' like mad. A man jumped out to stop him, but I knowed Garnett would niver stop this side o' th' gangway av his ship, an' sure 'nuff, out flashes his hand an' th' Dago rolls over an' over. They yelled harder than ever, an' Garnett had to shake out another reef afore he could make th' gang-plank, an' get aboard. He managed to get below jest as some soldiers rushed up. Th' noise brought Andrews on deck in time to get men to keep th' crowd off his ship, an' thin O'Toole comes up.

"'What's th' row?' he bawls to th' mate, but O'Toole ware laffin' so he couldn't spake a whurd. Finally he got it out.

"'Faith, 'tis th' leddy-killer av th' fleet, Garnett, at his owld game,' sez he. "Pon me whurd, 'tis a hangin' matter this time, fer th' damage he's done th' sex. He ware—' but he bruk down afore he could finish.

"'Twas five minits afore he could tell what had happened, th' old gal cussin' an' swearin' an' th' crowd a-hootin' an' jeerin', but finally th' skipper got some soldiers to carry th' old gal away. Thin out comes Garnett on th' main deck a-smellin' av his little vial, but avoidin' av th' skipper's eye.

"'What th' devil did ye mean?' asked Andrews; 'did ye take her to be Jameson in disguise?'

"'Pon me whurd,' says O'Toole, 'th' first wan that comes aboard was no other—an' this one looked enough like him from a stern view. 'Tis a bad trade, though, this killin' av leddies.' An' he leered so at Garnett he swore horrible an' went forrads.

"I ware standin' close enough to catch th' glint in Andrews' eye whin this ware said, but he took no notice an' went ashore, an' as I followed after him he was thinkin' hard."

Here Chips spat quietly into the corner, fingered his pipe, and rammed the ash down. Then he looked up at the light, and a different expression came upon him. The bos'n's smile died away, and all sat listening for the finish. Far forward sounded the cries of men dressing down the head sheets.

"I hadn't much to do," continued Chips, softly, "so I walked on an' saw him stop at a flower stand an' buy a bunch av roses. I wint across to th' cemetery where th' trees are good to look at an' th' grass is green as th' sea nigh th' States. I hadn't gone far whin I sees a man standin' nigh a grave wid another man lyin' on it. I couldn't tell who th' men ware till I came close, fer 'twas now gettin' dark. Thin when Andrews stooped an' lifted th' head av th' one lyin' down, I saw them both plain enough. Jameson's head made me feel sick wid th' horror av it. Whin I spoke, Andrews let th' poor fellow sink back again, an' as I stood alongside I saw th' flowers th' skipper had bought lyin' on th' grave nigh th' hand av poor Jameson, which still held his pistil. Th' old man said nothin', but there ware a hard look in his eyes as I saw him lookin' at th' tops av th' big Chilean mountings where th' sunken sun made them a bloody red. He ware thinkin' hard, an' seemed to be watchin' a flock av vultures a-comin' over th' range, stringin' out in a long line av black specks. Thin all av a sudden he stooped an' picked up the flowers an' placed thim gentle like on th' head av the grave—'twas the only gentil thing I iver knew him to do—an' thin walked away without a word. That's th' last I saw av him until I shipped aboard here, for he cleared from Valparaiso th' next day."

"An' this is the beggar we're taking back to the States to be skipper of some American ship, maybe this same one, if he gets clear of the killing of his quartermaster off Melbourne," said the bos'n.

"An' that's the reason, by your leave, Mr. Rolling," said Jim, "I say it's best to go back again and deliver this man up to the proper authorities."

"As far as I'm concerned," I answered, "I would just as soon see him safe where the wind won't annoy him; but I'm not the skipper, and if you want to get any satisfaction you'll have to go aft."

"We did," said the bos'n; "we asked the old man, but he wouldn't hear of it, and Trunnell is with him."

"Trunnell is with him because he thinks it right," said Jim, with a shrewd look at me; "but if you were to try to persuade him, I believe he would come around all right."

"Why fo' not put him abo'ad the English ship, sah," put in the "doctor." "I votes we ax the ole man to put 'im abo'ad her."

All were agreeable to this proposition and decided to go aft the first thing in the morning watch. Jim stuck out for going back.

"If you were to go with us, Mr. Rolling, we might persuade Trunnell," said he.

"It's no use, he never would—" Before we could continue the discussion further the bells struck out loudly, and the bos'n and I went on deck for our watch.

It was a fine, clear night, and I was glad to get the course from the mate and walk fore and aft on the weather side of the poop to enjoy it.

X

The morning dawned calm and beautiful. The heavy, oily swell, which still ran from the effects of the blow, moved in long, smooth humps upon the sea. Far to the eastward the light of the rising sun tinted the cirrus clouds above with a rosy hue.

I was quite tired from the effects of the gale, and the morning watch is always a cheerless one. The steward had coffee ready, however, and after a good drink I felt better, and got out the glass to see if I could make out the *Sovereign*. We had been drifting all night, so that in the mid-watch Trunnell wore ship and stood up for her to keep in sight. There she lay, about three miles away off our port beam. Her topsail was the only canvas she had set, and she was so low in the water that I could not see her deck amidships at that distance. All except a little of her high poop appeared to be under, or so low that it was invisible. I wondered why her captain had not put off sooner, and I knew that as soon as Thompson came on deck he would be in a fury at his having waited so long. There was not a breath of air now, so we were certain to be in company for several hours at least.

While I looked over the expanse of heaving ocean I saw a black spot between the ships. In a moment I made out a boat rising and falling, propelled by four oars, and headed for us. Sometimes she would disappear behind a high lump of sea and then she would be on top, and I made out she was coming along right handily.

As she drew nearer I made her out to be full of men. She came up under our mizzen channels and hailed. Half the watch was bending over the side looking at her, and one man threw a line. This was seized, and the next moment her crew came clambering over the rail.

Jenks, the old sailor who had come over in the boat with me the day before, was on deck to receive his shipmates. The old fellow's face wrinkled with amusement at the sight of his worn-out countrymen until it looked like the slack of a bellows. There was an unholy twinkle in his eye as he greeted them.

On the boarding of the officer of the boat, a tall Englishman who was the ship's mate, the man Jenks stopped his pleasantry at the tired crew's expense, but it was too late. He was ordered into the boat, with three other men who were fresh, to be sent away for the remaining men on the ship. Then the officer mounted the poop just as Captain Thompson emerged from below.

The officer bowed and touched his hat deferentially, but the skipper stood looking at him out of his glinting eyes, while his nose worked and twitched.

"Don't seem to be in much of a hurry, hey?" said our captain, with his drawl.

"We've been working steadily all night at the pumps, sir, hopin' to keep her afloat, sir. The old man—I beg pardon, Captain Sackett,—says as he'll not abandon her while she swims. The rest of us have permission to go, sir."

"Is her cargo of any particular value, then?"

"Yes, sir. It's palm oil and valuable woods. There's eight hundred barrels of palm oil in her, and the captain's got his all—every cent he has in the world. He won't leave her."

"Do you know what you resemble, hey?" said our skipper, dryly.

"I do not, sir."

"Well, I don't want to hurt the feelings of a poor, shipwrecked sailor, nor insinuate nothing sech as no gentleman ought. No, sirree. You are my guest aboard here, and damned welcome to you. At the same time, if I ware telling anybody as to what kind of a fellow you was, I should say,—yessir, after thinking the matter over carefully, and taking all points into consideration,— I might say that I thought ye an all-around white-livered, cowardly cuss, an' that's a fact."

The English mate turned red. He started to say something, and then checked himself. Finally he blurted out:—

"I've heard tell of some Yankee skippers who've given a bad name to your infernal shipping, an' I reckon I've run up against one. But no fear! I recognize you as our saviour, an' won't say a word, sir. The retort courteous, as the saying is, would be a crack on the jaw of such a fellow, but I don't say as I'll do it, sir. There's some fellows as needs rippin' up the back, but you bein' captain of this here ship, I won't say who they is, sir. No, sir, I won't say who they is, or nothin'. I just ask that I be sent back aboard the *Sovereign*. The boat ain't gone yet, and, by the Lord, I'll drown before I get into a ship like this."

"Well, by hookey, you won't, then," snarled the captain; "you'll stay aboard this boat. A man that's born to be hung mustn't be drowned. Hey, there, Rolling," he bawled, looking forward to where I stood, "get out the boat and go with those fellows. Get all the rest afeard to stay aboard, and come back. We won't stay here all day waiting for a lot of fellows too afeard to know what they want."

The noise of the talking brought a female figure to the combings of the companionway, and as the skipper finished, Miss Sackett stood on deck.

The mate of the *Sovereign* greeted her, and told of her father's determination to stay aboard his ship with three men who desired the chance to make heavy salvage. He didn't suppose any of the crew of the *Pirate* cared to take chances, but if they did, he would let them. He said he could work the wreck into some port, probably Cape Town, and save her.

"But he will surely be lost," cried Miss Sackett. "I shall go to him myself and persuade him not to do this foolish thing. You will let me go in one of the boats, won't you, Captain Thompson?" she cried, turning to our skipper.

Thompson was sour, but he admired nerve. The fact of the Englishman staying alone aboard his wrecked ship appealed to him where nothing else would.

"My dear madam," said he, with his drawl, "you shall certainly do jest what you want to while I'm captain of this boat. But I wouldn't persuade your father to do anything against his will. How could a sensible fellow refuse you anything, hey?"

The young girl overlooked his insolence, and smiled her satisfaction. She came forward to where the first boat was getting ready to shove off. The men in her were sullen and ugly, for they had not had their breakfast, and the row would be a long one. The old sailor, Jenks, with his pop eyes, and face like the slack of a bellows, scowled sourly. At this moment our third officer came on deck and to the lady's side. I was just about to ask her to wait and go in my boat when I heard the shrill tones of our Mr. Bell.

"Clear that boat, and stand by to pass this lady aboard," said he, with some show of authority, and a clever nautical style. "Allow me?" he continued, as he offered her his arm at the ladder.

His shrill voice caused a smile of wonder and amusement among the strangers, but as they knew their own skipper's daughter, they said nothing besides a few remarks among themselves.

"Won't you wait and have breakfast before you go," he asked her, as she reached the top of the rail; but she refused, and decided that her father's strange whim to stay aboard his sinking ship deserved first consideration.

"In that case I shall have to go along also, for you may be very much exhausted before getting back."

Just what good he could do in such a case he did not stop to explain, but climbed over the side, and after lowering her aboard, took his place beside her in the stern sheets. Then he gave orders to get clear, and the boat shot away, while I made shift to get my men something to eat before taking the long pull.

In fifteen minutes we were ready to start. Chips wanted to go along to see if anything could be done to help stop the leak in case Captain Sackett still insisted staying aboard. Johnson, the little sailor with the thin legs set wide apart, showing daylight between clear to his waist, Hans, the heavy-shouldered Swede, and Phillippi, a squat Dago, made up the rest of the boat's crew. Trunnell had come on deck while we were eating from the mess-kids, and met the skipper on the poop, where he stopped to talk over some important matter. This importance appeared to increase in a moment, for the skipper swore harshly and pointed forward just as my men were coming aft to go over the side.

"Rolling," he cried, "hold on with that boat a minute, and lay aft here," I came to the edge of the poop.

"Get that ruffian Andrews ready and put him aboard the *Sovereign*. The men here are tired of his ways, and fair exchange is no robbery. We'll take their men, they'll take one of ours, hey? Do you rise to that?"

I understood. The men had made it apparent they did not wish to have the fellow aboard since he persisted in his murderous ways. The skipper had been importuned by Jim to turn back and put him ashore. This he would not think of doing, but to propitiate them he had struck upon this new method of getting rid of his charge.

I called Jim, the young landsman, to lend a hand getting the fellow ready. Andrews cursed us all around and demanded to know what we were going to do with him. No attention was paid to him, however, and he was bundled into the boat, handcuffed, with his legs free.

"Tell Captain Sackett I say he's welcome to him," drawled out Thompson, over the poop rail. "Good luck to you, Andrews," he continued; "you'll have a pleasant voyage with no enemies to rip and cut. So long!"

This drew forth a volley of oaths from Andrews, but the skipper smiled, and we were soon out of earshot.

"What do you make of the weather, sir?" asked Jim, who pulled stroke oar. I looked over the smooth, heaving surface of the quiet ocean, and there was not the first sign of a breeze anywhere. The sun was partly obscured in a thick haze which seemed to come from everywhere and fill the entire atmosphere. The first boat was almost aboard the wreck, and we could see her looking like a black speck in the distance.

"It looks as though it might come on thick," I answered Jim, "but there's no danger of our parting company with the *Pirate* yet. There isn't enough wind to move her a knot an hour."

It was a long, hard pull to the *Sovereign* and when we arrived her captain was on deck with his daughter. She had finished trying to persuade him to leave his fortune, and stood near our third officer, who was ready to start back with the remainder of the crew. All but four men had insisted on leaving. These were the steward, two quartermasters, and a sailor.

"If there is any valuable stuff in the way of currency or spices, you can turn them over to me, and our captain will give you his receipt for them," I said, as I came over the side.

The little Englishman looked slowly up and down my six feet and more of length as I stood on the rail, and I fancied he smiled slightly. He was a florid-faced, bearded man, with clear blue eyes which had no sign of fear in them.

"I reckon we'll risk taking in what we have," said he; "at the same time I want to thank your captain for standing by and taking the men he has already. You don't think he could spare a few volunteers to help me in, do you? I'll give a hundred pounds to every man who'll stand by and run the risk."

"Well," I stammered, "I'm second mate myself, and therefore can't very well leave; but he's sent you one extra hand. The fellow is a good enough sailor, but he's in irons for fighting. He wants you to take him in exchange for the men you've sent."

The florid face of the English captain grew redder. His blue eyes seemed to draw to small points that pricked my inner consciousness. I suppose I showed some of my embarrassment, for he spoke in a gentler tone than I expected.

"Sir. I keep no one in peril against his wish. Neither do I run a convict ship. You may take your desperado back to your captain with the compliments of Captain Sackett, once of Her Majesty's Naval Reserve, and tell him the laws of his country are sufficient to deal with all persons."

"If I did," I answered, "you would have your men forced back into your wrecked vessel." And I pointed to the main deck, upon which the sea rolled and swashed in little foamy waves through the side ports, which were now below the heave of the swell. She was clear under amidships, and only the topgallant forecastle and poop were out of water, which was now nearly level with the floor in the after cabin. Everything showed wreck and ruin, from the splintered spars and tangled rigging to the yellow-white gaps in her bulwarks where the masts had crashed through.

"The will of the Lord is not to be set aside," he went on, with solemn and pious cheerfulness. "I would not risk so many lives for a man in irons. If, however, he will recognize the laws of the Almighty, I shall turn him adrift and trust that my mercy will not meet with ingratitude. You had better get my men ready, and if you can, take the trunks and cabin fixings in a boat. They might come to wrong here. My daughter will show where the things are I should like saved. As for myself, I shall stay where duty calls me, and will take this ship into some port and save her cargo, or go down in her. If I lose her, I lose my all, and with a wife and family I had better be gone with it. The Lord will temper the wind to the shorn lambs."

I called to Hans and Johnson to pass up the prisoner, and he soon stood on the *Sovereign's* poop, where he glared around him and made some inaudible remarks. The third mate, who stood near by, was about to speak to him when Captain Sackett stepped forward.

"My man," said he, "your captain has asked me to keep you here and help me work this ship in. You've been a master yourself, they tell me, so you will appreciate my difficulty. The Lord, however, always helps those who help themselves, and with his help we will land this vessel safe in port."

Andrews looked at the stout skipper sourly for a moment. Then he gave a deep snort and spat vulgarly upon the deck at his host's feet.

"What kind o' damn fool have I run up ag'in now, hey?" he mused in a low tone, as though speaking to himself, while he looked the skipper over. "Am I dreamin', or do I eternally run up ag'in nautical loonatic asylums? That's the question."

"My dear fellow, you don't seem to relish the fact that you must serve aboard here," said Sackett. "There's nothing irrational in trying to save a vessel when it's your plain duty to do so. The Lord sometimes dismasts us to try us. We must not give up our duty because we have hardships to encounter. Your captain cannot take care of so many people, probably, and wishes you to stay here with me. If you will pass your word to do your share of the work, as I believe you will, I shall cast off those irons this instant and put you second in command. There will then be five of us, all able-bodied men, to get her in to the Cape."

"Of all the slumgullion I ever had stick in my craw, this beats me," observed the prisoner, in his even tone, without taking his eyes off Sackett. "I pass my word, an' you turn me loose to do my duty. Well—say, old man, can you tell me of a miracle you reads out o' your Bible? I wants to make a comparison." Here he gave a loud snort and grinned. "There's an old sayin' that any port is good in a storm," he went on, "an' likewise any ship in a calm. I rise to it, old man. I'll be your mate; for, if things ain't all gone wrong, I'll sail straight inter Heaven with ye. Cast me loose."

"It shall be done at once," said Sackett. "I shall request, sir," said he, turning to me, "that the irons be stricken off your man."

I told Chips to go ahead and cut them, and then followed Miss Sackett and the third mate below, to get what belongings they wanted sent aboard the *Pinto* to be kept clear of water.

"It's a pity papa will do this absurd thing," said Miss Sackett, impetuously, as she landed upon the cabin deck. I was following close behind her on the companion and hastened to cheer her.

"There's not much danger," I said; "for the vessel can't possibly sink with all the oil and wood in her. He will probably bring her in all right and save many thousands of dollars. Maybe the carpenter can find the leak and plug it. In that case she'll be as sound as a dollar and safe as a house, when they get her pumped."

"I don't know about it," she answered; "I feel that papa is going to his death, and I know that if mamma finds out he won't leave, she'll come back aboard. Here is one trunk. That chest under the berth is to go also. I'll get what clothes I can gather up, and bring them along in a bundle. Goodness! hear the water slapping about under the deck; it is perfectly dreadful to think of any one staying aboard a ship half sunk like this."

The steward, a very clever-looking young man with a brown mustache, helped us get the things on deck, where they were taken in charge by the rest of the men, seven in number, who were going with us.

While we were below, Chips, after cutting Andrews adrift, tried to find out where the leak was located. The vessel's hold was so full of water, however, that he gave up the search. Only a survey of her bilge outside would help clear up matters, and allow work upon it.

Captain Sackett had taken an observation and had figured himself out to be within six hundred miles of Cape Town. He was very thankful for our kindness and stood near by, wishing us all kinds of good luck, while the things were being lowered over the ship's low side. In a few minutes all hands were called to get into the *Pirate's* boat, the one of the *Sovereign* being left for the safety of those on board. Miss Sackett took a tearful farewell of her father, and was placed aft. Then we shoved off, and were soon leaving the half-sunken ship astern.

"Cap'n," said Jenks, who sat aft near me, "what d'ye make o' that?"

He pointed to a white bank of vapor which had rolled up from the southward, and suddenly enveloped the *Sovereign* while we were still two cable lengths distant. I looked and saw the white mist, which we had not noticed before to be so dense, rolling in long white clouds upon the calm surface of the ocean. In a moment it had enveloped us, and all around us was a white wall, the *Pirate* disappearing ahead. The swell also appeared to be getting a cross roll to it, and a light air now blew in our faces.

I made no answer to the leather-faced sailor, but tried to keep the boat's head before a heavier roll of the sea, and the wake as much like a straight line as possible. There was no compass in the craft, and it would take some nice guesswork to find a ship three miles away.

XI

We went along in silence for some time, the fog seeming to fall like a pall upon the spirits of the men. The wash of the oars and the gurgle of the bow-wave were the only sounds that were audible. After half an hour of this I arose and sent a hail through the bank of mist, which I thought would reach a vessel within half a mile. There was no sound of an answer, the dank vapor appearing to deaden my hail and swallow up all noise a short distance beyond the boat. It was uncanny to feel how weak that yell appeared. I saw Jim looking at me with a strange light in his eyes as though he felt danger in the air.

After an hour more of it, the faces of the men plainly showed their anxiety. Phillippi, the Dago, was chewing the corner of his dank mustache, and his eyes wandered aft and then forward. Jenks, with his large wrinkled face gray with the vapor, sat staring ahead, straining his ears for the slightest sound that would locate the vessel. I put both hands to my mouth again, and strained away my hardest. There was no response, the sound falling flat and dull in the wall of mist. Then I knew we were in danger, and gave the order to stop rowing.

The silence around us was now oppressive. We were all waiting to hear some sound that would locate either one or the other of the vessels. The breeze carried the masses of vapor in cool spurts into our faces, and I felt sure the *Pirate* would soon change her bearings under its influence. We had been running away from the main heave of the sea, as I supposed, but now there appeared to be a sidelong motion running with the swell and at an angle to its general direction.

"'Tis no manner av use tryin' to keep along as we are, d'ye think so?" suggested Chips. "We must have passed her."

I hailed again, and after waiting for an answer, headed the boat around in the hope that we had overreached the ship, and would come within hailing distance on our way back. The order was given to pull very easily, and listen for sounds.

"This is most disgusting," said Miss Sackett. "I'm as hungry as a bear, and here we'll be out for the Lord only knows how long. I think you might have seen to it that I had some breakfast." And she looked at Mr. Bell, our third officer.

"There's water under the stern sheets," suggested that officer, meekly. But the young lady gave a pretty pout, and shrugged her shoulders.

In a little while we stopped again and hailed loudly. The only sound in answer was the low hiss of a sea, which had begun to make with the breeze, and which broke softly ahead.

Suddenly we heard the distant clang of a ship's bell. It sounded far away to starboard.

"Give way, bullies, strong," I cried, and the next instant we were heading toward it. Then it died away, and we heard it no more.

After ten minutes' pull, we stopped again, for fear of overreaching our mark. We hailed and got no answer. Then we rowed slowly along, listening in the hope they would ring again. In a little while we lay drifting, and all hands strained their ears for sound.

Suddenly something alongside gave a loud snort. I started up, and the men turned their faces forward. A deeper shadow seemed to hang over us, and the breeze died away. Then the snort was repeated, and a voice spoke forth:—

"Of all the damned fools I ever see, that second mate stands way ahead. Now I onct thought Trunnell didn't know nothin', but that young whelp is a pizenous fool, an' must be ripped up the back. Sackett, old man, your daughter can't leave ye. Here she be alongside with them boatmen agin."

The voice was drawling and not loud, but I recognized it fast enough.

In an instant the boat's bow struck the side of the *Sovereign*, and we saw Andrews leaning over the rail near us, looking down with a sour smile.

There was nothing to do but go aboard, for we had nothing to eat in the small boat, and the danger of getting lost entirely was too great to make another attempt to get back to the *Pirate* while the fog lasted.

Miss Sackett was helped over the rail by her father, who came up immediately, and the rest scrambled over with some choice English oaths as they commented upon their luck. Andrews gave me a queer look as I climbed past him, and for an instant I was ready to spring upon him. But he gave a snort of disgust and turned away.

Chips, Jim, and the others of our crew came aboard, and the small boat was dropped astern where she towed easily, the breeze just giving the sunken ship steering way under the storm topsail.

The beef barrels were in no way injured by their immersion in salt water, so Captain Sackett gave the steward orders to prepare a meal for all hands upon the cabin stove. Salt junk and tinned fruits were served for everybody who cared to eat them, and afterward all hands felt better. The ship's water-tanks were full of good water, and no one listed considerably to starboard under the

- 72 -

gentle breeze, owing to her water-logged condition, the port tank was accessible from the deck pipe.

I had enough to eat before coming out, and the predicament we were in did not tend to strengthen my appetite. I, however, made out to sit down at the cabin table with Captain Sackett, Andrews, who was now his mate, and our third officer. Miss Sackett joined us, and we fell to.

No sooner had Andrews started to shovel in the good junk, and Mr. Bell the fruit, than Sackett arose from the table and looked severely down upon them. Fortunately, my satisfied appetite had prevented any unnecessary hurry to eat on my part, for our new skipper frowned heavily.

"I wish to give thanks, O Lord," said he, raising his eyes toward the skylight and dropping his voice into a dignified tone, "for thy kind mercy in delivering us from the perils of the deep. Make us duly thankful for thy mercy and for the food thou hast seen fit to place before us."

"Amen," sounded a gruff voice beside me.

I looked at Andrews, but he appeared to pay no attention whatever to what was transpiring. Then I turned to Sackett to see if he had taken offence.

The stout, ruddy-faced skipper seemed to be changed to stone for an instant, and his fixed glare was full upon Andrews.

The ruffian appeared to enjoy the situation, for he gave a fierce snort and turned his face to the skipper.

"No offence, old man, sit down and eat your grub. There's no use working up unchristian-like feeling between us simply because I'm not going to let any damn foolishness stand between me and my vittles. Eat while ye may, says I, and God bless you for a kind-hearted, gentle skipper. You says yourself that the Lord helps them as helps themselves, which goes to show I'll just make a stab for another piece o' that junk before some other son of a gun runs afoul of it an' helps himself. Which would be goin', o' course, agin the will o' the Lord."

Sackett hardly breathed. His face turned purple with rage. Andrews took no notice of him save to draw a revolver from his pocket and place it on the table beside his plate.

"Sit down and eat, papa," said Miss Sackett, who was at his right hand, and as she did so she placed her hand upon his shoulder.

The touch of his daughter's hand seemed to bring the skipper back to his senses, or rather seemed to enable him to thrust his present feelings aside for her sake. He sat down and stared at Andrews for fully a minute, while that ruffian ate and winked ofttimes at Mr. Bell. Once in a while he would give a loud snort and hold his face upward for an instant. Then a sour smile would play around his ugly mouth as though he enjoyed his humor intensely. The third officer frowned severely at him several times, and then asked in his silly voice if he would please behave himself.

The effect was altogether too ludicrous to be borne. Miss Sackett smiled in spite of herself and I almost laughed outright. Then, feeling sorry for my host, I began to eat as an excuse to hide my feelings. Sackett ate little, and in silence. When he was through, he arose and left for the deck, leaving the rest of us at the table. Miss Sackett followed him quickly, as though she instinctively felt what might happen if she remained.

I sat there looking at Andrews for some moments. He raised his head several times and gave forth his peculiar snort, smiling at Mr. Bell. "Young fellow," said he, slowly, "we've had a turn or two, an' nothin' much has come of it. Let's shake an' call it square." And he held out his hand toward me.

"I suppose you really had some cause to lose your temper," I answered, "the day I hailed you from the poop, because you were used to commanding there. I've heard many unpleasant things about you, Captain Andrews, but if you will let matters pass, I'm willing. I never turned down a man yet on hearsay when he was willing to see me half way."

Here I took his hard, muscular hand and held it for a moment. He smiled sourly again, but said no more about our fight.

"Ye see," he went on, after a moment's pause, "I'm second in command here now, and I'll show you no such treatment like what I got aboard the *Pirate*. This gun I has here is only to let a man see his limit afore it's too late. If I didn't show it, he might go too far, and then—well, I reckon ye know just what might happen, being as Trunnell has told you what a gentle, soft-hearted fellow I am. He's a rum little dog, that fuzzy-headed fellow, Trunnell. Did ye ever see sech arms in anything but an ape? 'Ell an' blazes, he could squeeze a man worse than a Coney Island maiden gal. Speakin' of maidens, jest let me hint a minute in regard to the one aboard here. She's a daisy. An out an' out daisy. An' if there's a-goin' to be any love-makin' going on around, I'll do it. Yes, sir, don't take any of my duties upon yourself. I'll do it. I'll do it. Jest remind yourself of that, Mr. Rolling, an' we'll get along fust rate. The old man don't know me yet, but Mr. Bell here—well, Mr. Bell knows a thing or two concernin' captains which'll be worth a heap of gold to some people."

The third mate looked at me with his boyish eyes for an instant, and his ruddy cheeks seemed to blush. Then he said softly:—

"What he means is, that you and the rest are only passengers, now. All the men from the *Pirate*, you know. There'll be some salvage for the four who elected to stay aboard this vessel, and if you understand it in this light, you,

Chips, Jim, and the rest are welcome as passengers. If you don't, the boat is at your disposal any time."

"I see," I said. "You are also of the party elected to stay with Captain Sackett and draw salvage?"

"That's about the size of it."

I went on deck, and Chips, Jim, and the men went below to get something to eat. Sackett was standing at the break of the poop as I came up, and his daughter stood beside him. They were evidently in earnest conversation over the scene below, for as I drew near, Miss Sackett turned to me and said with some show of contempt in her voice:—

"Your captain was very kind to send us your volunteer, and we appreciate it, Mr. Rolling. Perhaps the reason he had no more men offer their services for a dangerous mission was because he was short of irons."

"If you mean that American sailors have to be ironed into danger, you are mistaken," I answered, somewhat nettled. "However, I quite agree with you in regard to this one as an awkward fellow. Better wait and see how he acts in time of danger before condemning him."

I had not the heart to tell her what a ruffian they had turned loose upon her father. It would do little good, for Sackett had passed his word to make Andrews second in command, and I knew from what I had seen of this religious skipper, that he would keep it at any cost. As for Chips, myself, and the rest of the men, seven of the *Sovereign's* crew and ourselves, we were simply passengers, as Mr. Bell had informed us. We had no right whatever to take any part in affairs aboard, for the salvage would fall to those who elected to stay.

Captain Sackett moved away from me as I stood talking to his daughter and showed he did not wish to discuss Andrews. He went to the edge of the poop and stared down on the main deck where the water surged to and fro with the swell. He had a badly wrecked ship under him, and there was little time to lose getting her in better condition, for a sudden blow might start to break her up, or roll the seas over her so badly that no one could live aboard.

I stood for some minutes talking to the young girl, and when her father spoke to me she held out her hand, smiling. "We'll be shipmates now and you'll have a chance to show what a Yankee sailor can do. I believe in heroes— when they're civil," she added.

"Unfortunately for the worshipper of heroes, there is a great deal left to the goddess Chance, in the picking of them," I answered. "Admiration for human beings should not be hysterical."

"From the little I've seen of men during the six voyages I've made around the world in this ship with papa, your advice is somewhat superfluous," she said, with the slightest raising of the eyebrows. Then she went aft to the taffrail and stood gazing into the fog astern.

"Mr. Rolling," said Sackett, "there's no use of thinking about leaving the ship while the fog lasts, now. You might have made the *Pirate* by close reckoning before, but she must have changed her bearings fully a half a dozen points since you started. She's under canvas, and this breeze will send her along at least six knots and drift her two with her yards aback. You might as well take hold here and get some of your men to lend a hand. The foremast is still alongside, and we might get a jury rig on her without danger of heeling her on her bilge. She's well loaded, the oil and light stuff on top, so she won't be apt to turn turtle."

It was as he said. We were all in the same ship, so as to speak, wrecked and water-logged to the southward of the Cape. The best thing to do was to take it in the right spirit and fall to work without delay, getting her in as shipshape condition as possible. The fog might last a week, and the *Pirate* might get clear across the equator before stopping a second time in her course. I knew that even Trunnell would not wait more than a few hours; for if we did not turn up then, it was duff to dog's-belly, as the saying went, that we wouldn't heave in sight at all. The ocean is a large place for a small boat to get lost in, and without compass or sextant there would be little chance for her to overhaul a ship standing along a certain course.

The dense vapor rolled in cool masses over the wreck, and the gentle breeze freshened so that the topsail, which still drew fair from the yard, bellied out and strained away taut on a bowline, taking the wind from almost due north, or dead away from the Cape. The *Sovereign* shoved through it log-wise under the pull, the swell roaring and gurgling along her sunken channels and through her water ports. She was making not more than a mile an hour, or hardly as fast as a man could swim, yet on she went, and as she did so, she was leaving behind our last hope of being picked up.

XII

The first night we spent aboard the hulk was far from convincing us of her seaworthiness. I had been in—a sailor is never "on board"—two ships that had seen fit to leave me above them, but their last throes were no more trying to the nerves than the ugly rooting of the *Sovereign* into the swell during that night. At each roll she appeared to be on the way to turn her keel toward the sky, and, at a plunge slowly down a sea-slope, she made us hold our breaths. Down, down, and under she would gouge, the water roaring and seething over sunken decks amidships, and even pouring over the topgallant rail until it would seem certain she was making her way to the bottom, and I would instinctively start to rise from the cabin transom to make a break for the deck. Then she would finally stop and take a slow heave to windward, which started a Niagara thundering below the deck, where the cargo was torn loose and sent crashing about in a whirlpool.

I once read a description by an English landsman of a shipwreck, and he told how the water would rest for an instant level with the rail, seeming to pause motionless for a fraction of a second before flowing over and sinking the ship, I lay a long time wondering vaguely at an imagination that could make such a description possible, and as a heaving swell would start along the rail at the waist, and go thundering along in a roaring surf the entire length of the midship section over the edge, fetching up with a crash against the forward cabin bulkhead, I heartily wished the writer were aboard to share our sufferings. There was no spoon and teacup business about that ship, and it sometimes seemed as though seven or eight seas were rolling over her rails from all directions at once.

We were still below the thirty-eighth parallel, and consequently the morning broke early, for it was January and midsummer. I arose from the transom and went on deck at dawn, and found that the fog had lifted. Andrews met me as I came from below, and gave me a nod as I took in the horizon line at a glance.

"I reckon old hook-nose didn't care to wait any longer," he growled sourly.

I took up the glass from the wheel box, and scanned the line carefully. There was not a thing in sight save the smooth swell, ruffled now by the slight breeze, and turning a deep blue-gray in the light of the early morning. The sun rose from a cloudless horizon and shone warmly upon the wreck. The foam glistened and sparkled in the rosy sunlight, and looking over the rail I could see deep down into the clear depths. The copper on the ship's bilge looked a light gray, and even the tacks were visible. She drifted slowly along with just steering way, and the spar alongside, which the men had tried to get aboard again, made a gurgling wake with its heel.

"What do you make of it, Chips?" I asked, as the carpenter waded out in the waist and came up the poop ladder.

"Long cruise an' plenty o' water, that's about th' size av ut, don't ye think, sir?" the carpenter answered. "Trunnell has been took off, fer sure. I don't mind stickin' aboard th' bleedin' hooker if there was a chanst to get th' salvage; but no fear o' that while Andrews is here. He'll block any argument to divvy up. Seems as we might even get down under her bilge durin' this spell av weather, an' see where th' leak is located. 'Tis a butt started, most like. Them English stevedores generally rams th' stuffin' out av a ship in spite av th' marks they puts on 'em."

Captain Sackett came from below and joined us.

"I'd like to get that foremast aboard while it holds calm," said he; "and if you'll start the men, we'll have it done by noon. The sooner we all work together, the better. We ought to get sail on forward in less than a week, and then, with a jury topmast, make enough way to get in while the grub holds out."

The steward got breakfast in the after-cabin, and as soon as the men had eaten they were turned to rigging tackles to hoist the dragging foremast aboard. It was trailing by the lee rigging, which had held, and it had thumped and pounded along the ship's side to such an extent during the blow that several of her strakes were nearly punched through. It was a beautiful morning,—the blue sky overhead and the calm, blue ocean all around us. The men worked well, and even the sour ruffian, Andrews, who stood near and took charge of part of the work,—for he was an expert sailor,—seemed to brighten under the sun's influence. Chips went to work at the stump of the foremast, and cut well into it at a point almost level with the deck. This he fashioned into a scarf-joint for a corresponding cut in the piece of mast which had gone overboard. Tackles were rigged from the main-topmast head, and, by a careful bracing with guys forward and at both sides, the wreck of the foremast was slowly raised aboard.

The *Sovereign* forged ahead faster when relieved of this load. On the second day, when we had the foremast fished, and the yards, which had held to it, safe on deck, ready to be hoisted and slung again, we found that the vessel had made over seventy miles to the westward along the thirty-eighth parallel. This was over a mile an hour; but of course some of this drift was due to the edge of the Agullas current, which was setting somewhat to the southward and westward.

Andrews had little to say to me or to Chips. In fact, he appeared to be satisfied with his lot now that he seemed sure of getting salvage money. Only Jim, who seemed to have eyes everywhere, distrusted the man, and spoke to me about him. We had now been on the wreck five days, working and rigging away at the foremast, and the calm, beautiful weather held with no signs of a change. Jim was hanging over the side, resting his feet on the fore channels while he helped Chips to bolt in a deadeye which had been torn out when the mast had gone. The sun was warm and shone brilliantly, and Chips sweated and grunted as he pounded away at the iron. There were no other men in our immediate vicinity, so after pounding away in silence for a quarter of an hour, the carpenter spoke.

"'Tis bloody well we've been treated to get no share av the wreck, whin here we are sweatin' our brains out wid th' work av refittin'," said he.

"And what the devil is a few hundred pounds of salvage to me?" growled Jim, hot with his exertion. "See here, man! I've left ten thousand behind me on the *Pirate.*"

"And a pious regard fer the truth along wid it," added Chips, smiting the lug-bolt heavily.

Jim's face was so serious that I asked what he meant, and with the heat of the work upon him and the absolute hopelessness of ever getting back aboard our ship before his eyes, he spoke out:—

"Did you ever hear of Jackwell, the fellow who cracked the Bank of Sydney?" he asked.

Chips and I both admitted that we had. He was the most notorious burglar in the southern hemisphere.

"But what are ye askin' sich a question fer?" asked Chips. "What's burglars got to do wid losin' salvage?"

"He was aboard the *Pirate*, and a reward awaits the lucky dog who lands him. Just a trifle of ten thousand dollars," said Jim, fiercely.

Chips turned on him.

"Is it sure 'nuff truth ye're tellin', or jest a yarn to soothe our feelin's?" he demanded. "I don't call to mind any gallus-lookin' chap in th' watch."

"He never stood watch, and I wasn't certain of him until we were out to sea and it was too late. What d'ye suppose I tried to get Trunnell to go back for? 'Twas the old man, you stupid wood-splitter. You don't think I'm a sailor, do you?"

"'Pon me sowl, how cud I? I niver had th' heart to hurt yer feelings, Jim, me son, or ye'd have heard from me before. But what are ye, thin?" And Chips leaned back against the rail.

"Nothing but a——" and Jim opened his coat which he had always worn since coming aboard the *Pirate*. On the inside was a silver shield stamped handsomely with the insignia of the detective corps of Melbourne.

"A sea lawyer aboard a derelict. Ye do fairly well, considerin'. An' th' old man? You don't really mean it?"

"What?" I asked; "do you mean that Thompson's a burglar; and that he's Jackwell himself?"

"Nothing else, and I'm out for the reward, which I won't get now. You know now how he came aboard. If I'd only been a few hours sooner, it would have been all right. He was about to buy his passage when he found the real Captain Thompson wasn't there, and would probably not be down until the last minute. That was enough for him. Trunnell was taken clear aback by his nerve. It was a risky thing to do, but Jackwell takes risks. The man has more real cheek and impudence than any above ground, or water either, for that matter. He ain't much afraid of a fight when it comes to it, although he'd rather use his wits than his gun. That's just what makes me feel sore. But that isn't all. Andrews is going to get clear of some of us."

"He's tried it several times on me," I said, with a smile. "What makes you think he'll try again?"

"I heard enough of what was passing between that third mate and steward last night to know it. But I don't want to scare you fellows," he added, with a smile.

Chips gave a grunt of disgust, and I spat contemptuously over the side without further remark. Our manner was not lost on Jim. He sobered instantly.

"You know we're in the way aboard, if we land the hooker all right," he said slowly. "That's clear as mud. You know also that Trunnell and the rest aboard the *Pirate* know we don't belong here and haven't any right to stay except as passengers. Trunnell saw us put off in the boat. He could see us plainly when we started and was, of course, looking at us all the time until the fog closed in. You follow this lay, don't you?"

Chips and I nodded.

"Well, if the *Sovereign* turns up with our boat load missing and Sackett dead, she'll be in good evidence of what all hands aboard the *Pirate* saw, won't she?"

It dawned suddenly upon us that this was a fact. Trunnell and Thompson, and in fact all hands, were looking after us, waiting for us to come back aboard before swinging the yards and standing away again on our course. There wasn't a man aboard the *Pirate*, we felt certain, who had not seen the boat start away from the ship with our men and Miss Sackett aboard her, for they had nothing in the world to do but watch. Then they had seen the fog envelop us on our way. We had not turned up, and the only thing to infer, if the *Sovereign* came in without us, was that we had missed our way and had gone adrift in the southern ocean. The word of Andrews and the rest aboard the English ship could hardly be doubted under the circumstances. If we cut adrift in the small boat or were done away with as Jim suggested, our friends would be witnesses who would help our enemies by any testimony they might give.

Chips dropped his hammer and drew a hand across his forehead, thinking.

"What did the third mate say in regard to our going?" I asked Jim.

"I couldn't hear the talk, only part of a sentence whispered by that man-woman when the steward came into the cabin during the mid-watch last night with a can of salmon and some ship's bread. They stood near the door of the alleyway, talking, and I suddenly came bulging into them with rubber boots on. He said something about Andrews being a fine captain and perfectly capable of taking this ship in or out any port on the African coast. That's all."

I stopped serving the end of the lanyard I was at work on and looked across the deck to where Andrews stood with several men. His sinister face with its sour smile was turned toward us as though he studied our thoughts.

"You're not over busy, Mr. Rolling," said Sackett, coming along the rail to the rigging. "I wish you and the carpenter would try to get a gantline over the side and look along under her for the butt. In this clear water the chances are good for getting a sight of it if it's well up on her bilge. We ought to stop her up some while the calm lasts."

XIII

At noon Sackett came on deck to take the sun. His second officer, Journegan, a heavily built man with mutton-chop whiskers of a colorless hue, was incapable of the smallest attempt at navigation, so he stood idly by while his superior let the sun rise until it had reached its highest point.

"Eight bells," cried Sackett, and went below to work out the sight.

"By the grace of God," echoed Andrews, who had come upon the poop.

The second officer smiled at his attempted wit and struck off the bells. He appeared to be quite friendly with Andrews and stopped a moment afterward to chat with him.

When we went below to dinner the words of Jim were fresh in my mind. How would Andrews try to get clear of us? The fact that he intended to do it I firmly believed, for the ruffian had such a sinister character that I felt certain his only reason for being apparently satisfied at present was because he intended some treachery. What part the third officer of the *Pirate* would play in the affair I could hardly guess. Jim knew nothing about him, but since he came aboard with Thompson, there was every reason to believe that this rosy-cheeked youngster with the girl's voice was an accomplished villain. That Andrews and he understood each other was certain. Andrews was most blasphemous at meals, and would endeavor to engage Sackett in an argument concerning devils, hell, and many other subjects not relating to navigation of the Indian Ocean. At such times the third mate would raise his piping voice and plead with Andrews not to shock him with his profanity. The second officer of the *Sovereign* appeared to enjoy the situation, and would laugh until ordered from the table by Sackett. Miss Sackett, of course, would not dine with the rest, but had her meals served in her stateroom by the steward, who did it with a very bad grace, grumbling and complaining at the extra work. He was a good-looking young man, this steward, and the fact that he complained told plainly that there was something between the men that was doing away with discipline. The steward's name was Dalton, and he was a fair specimen of the London cockney. Stout and strong, he was as ignorant as an animal and about as easily persuaded into doing things as an obstinate mule. He was also about as hard to dissuade. The other men of the *Sovereign's* crew were Bull England, a powerful sailor who had served many years in the navy, and who was also a prize fighter, and Dog Daniels, a surly old fellow, who was continually growling at everything. He was six feet six inches and over in height, and as lean and gaunt as the white albatross hovering over our wake. Journegan, the second officer, made the last but not least of the select four who had elected to stay aboard with Sackett to take in the ship and get salvage.

If Andrews had weapons, which I had reason to believe he had since his show of a revolver upon the captain's table, there would be six armed men against thirteen and a woman, for I had no reason to doubt Sackett was to be done away with if the rest were.

I pondered while I ate the cold junk and ship's bread, listening to Andrews holding forth to Mr. Bell and Journegan upon the fallacy of trusting to a power that was highly unintelligible.

"For instance," said he, "for why should I give thanks fer this stinkin' junk meat when I don't know but what Dalton, there, has put his dirty hands on it an' pisened it fit to kill? How do I know if he washes his hands afore cookin', hey? Look at them warts an' tell me if they ain't ketchin'. Jest think of a stomach full o' warts. Is that anything to be thankful for, I'd like to know."

The idea amused Journegan, but it set me to thinking about the medicine chest in spite of myself. Sackett scowled while this sort of talk went on, but said nothing to bring forth an outbreak from Andrews. I wondered why he did not try to get his men with him and clap the fellow in irons. There was every reason to believe they would have obeyed him at first, but he hesitated for some religious purpose better known to himself, until the fellow had obtained such a sway over the crew that it was now doubtful if it could be done without an open fight between them and the men he had to back him.

Sackett announced to me that we had made no westing to speak of, on account of the ship now being in the southeasterly set of the Agullas current. We had drifted along with the topsail and two staysails drawing from the main, and a sort of trysail set from a preventer-stay leading aft. In spite of this amount of canvas the breeze had been so light that the sunken ship had not made a mile in two hours. It was disheartening, but if we could only get at the leak and stop some of the water from flowing into her, we might get her up a bit and then she would move faster. Her hatch-combings were high, and the sea had not washed clear over them yet, while her high strakes would be all the tighter, now that they had been under water for days. This seemed to be a very fair argument, but, while the skipper talked, my eyes were upon the glass case at the end of the cabin, where a row of bottles showed through the front and above the wooden frames. They contained the drugs usually carried aboard ship, and while the skipper talked to me I wondered if there were any poisons in that case which would be of service to Andrews. When we were through, the captain and I left the cabin, for there had been no watches at meals; all had eaten together in order to facilitate matters of cooking, the men only eating at different times from the officers.

As we passed up the after-companionway, I looked into the case and endeavored to interest the skipper in drugs for the men in case of sickness.

He showed me a bottle of arnica, one of squibbs, another of peppermint, and many other drugs used as simple remedies. At the end of a long row was one containing a white powder, unlabelled. I picked it up and opened the vial, thinking to taste it to see if it was quinine. Its weight, however, made me certain this could not be, and I was just about to put a bit on my tongue when Sackett stopped me.

"It's bichloride of mercury. Don't taste it," said he.

I was not much of a chemist; for a mate's knowledge of the atomic theory must necessarily be slight.

"What's that?" I asked.

"Oh, a poison. I only keep it for vermin and certain skin diseases. It's too deadly to keep around, though, and I've a notion to heave it overboard—"

"Steamer on starboard quarter, sir," came the cry of England, who was at the wheel.

We were bounding up the companionway in an instant, and looking to the northward as soon as our feet struck the deck. There, sure enough, was a dark smudge of smoke on the horizon.

"Get the glass," said Sackett.

He took it and gazed hard at the dark streak.

"I can just make out her mastheads. She seems to be coming along this way,'" he said, after a moment.

All hands gathered upon the poop and watched the smoke. Those who hadn't had their dinner, hastily went below and came up again with the junk in their hands, munching it as they stood gazing after the rising mastheads. Soon the funnel of the steamer rose above the horizon, and showed that she was standing almost directly parallel to our course. We had run up a distress signal from the main, and now all waited until the stranger should make it out and send a boat or heave to. Our own boat was towing astern, so Sackett had her drawn up to the mizzen channels, ready for the men to get aboard. Miss Sackett came from below and announced that she was ready to accompany the boat.

"If you are silly enough to stay, papa, I can't help it," she said. "I am tired of sitting around in a cabin with my feet in the water, eating stuff fit for pigs. I think you really ought to give the old boat up."

"So do I, Missy," said Andrews. "I can't think of any good a-coming to the old man by staying aboard a craft half sunken like this one. I think your girl is giving you good advice, Captain Sackett."

- 84 -

"I think you heard me state just how I felt about the matter, Mr. Andrews," replied the captain. "If you're disposed to quit, you can go in the boat."

"Oh, no," said the ruffian, "I intend to stay." And he lent such emphasis to the last word that Sackett gave him a sharp glance to see if he meant anything more.

In half an hour the steamer was passing abreast, and we were in the boat rowing hard to head her off. We set a signal on our mast forward, and pulled desperately, but she never even slowed down, passing along half a mile distant on the calm ocean. She must have seen us, for the day was bright and cloudless as could be. We hailed and waved until she was a speck to the westward, leaving us alone again save for the sunken ship under our lee.

"It's just the way with a Dago," said Jenks. "They always leaves a fellow just when they shouldn't, and when I first seen that yaller flag I felt pretty sure we'd come in fer somethin' like this."

No one said anything further, for our disappointment was sharp. Even Phillippi, the Portuguese, took no offence at the allusion to Dagos, but rowed in silence back to the *Sovereign*.

"It seems like you can't leave us," said Andrews, sourly, when we returned. "There ain't much room aboard this hooker, an' I don't see why you forever turn back to her when you ain't wanted here."

Jenks climbed up the mizzen channels, which were now no higher than the boat's bow, and made the painter fast on deck without remark. Chips followed him closely.

"If ye mane there's no room aboard fer us, thin why in hell don't ye git out th' way an' rid th' ship av a useless ruffian," said the Irishman.

Andrews scowled at him, but changed his look into a sour smile.

"By the grace of the good Lord, I never rips up a sailor for slack jaw aboard the Lord's special appointed ship. Maybe we'll settle the matter of leaving later on," said the ruffian.

"Let there be an end of this talk, sir," said Sackett. "Get your men to work, Mr. Andrews, and you, Mr. Rolling, get the passengers out of that boat and stand by to try to find the leak. I don't intend to have any more of this eternal bickering."

Miss Sackett was helped aboard again. As she stepped on deck she whispered, "There's no use, Mr. Rolling. We will have to get out. The only trouble is that the water is gaining slowly in the cabin, and I'm afraid for papa."

"It's a pity he won't desert her," I answered; "but if we get away, Andrews and the rest will be more apt to help him honestly. They won't while we're here, and he won't force any of his men to stay and obey orders, as he should. If he only would, we might get the ship in before a week more of it."

"It's his way," said the girl. "He believes no captain has the right to endanger his men for gain. You couldn't take him by force, for he'd make things warm after he got ashore. If we could only get some of the water out of her and get away, he could get her in with England, Journegan, Daniels, and Dalton. Your two men added would make seven. These men could handle the canvas and steer her as well as twelve."

I didn't like to tell her that the devil himself would hardly be safe in the same ship with Andrews. It was quite possible that the ruffian would turn to and do good work for his share of the salvage when he got clear of the rest of us, for the amount would be large and tempting. Sackett would be of more service to him alive than dead.

"We'll get at the leak this afternoon, if it's possible," I said, and the young girl went back to her stateroom.

XIV

It was with anything but rising spirits that Chips went at the leak. He had a frame slung outboard some fifteen feet from the ship's side, supported by guys from the mainmast and jury foremast. It was after eight bells in the afternoon before this was finished, and then Sackett and he went out on it to study the ship's bilge through the calm water. It was almost flat calm, but the *Sovereign* had steering way enough to turn her side to the slanting sun, letting the light shine under her copper. She was so deep, however, nothing could be made out on the smooth green surface that showed like a started plank end. Only here and there a lump or protuberance appeared, showing a bunch of marine growth, or a bent edge of a plate where it had started to rip off. The water of the Indian Ocean is always remarkably clear, and this day during the still weather it was like liquid air. Objects were as distinctly visible three or four fathoms below the surface as those at a corresponding distance on deck.

I joined Sackett and Chips on the frame, and studied the ship's bilge the entire length of her waist. In about half an hour we shifted to starboard and, by dint of handling the canvas, got her head around so that the sun shone under this side. Nothing showed like a leak.

"If a man could dive under her a few times," said Sackett, "he might see, with the light as good as it is now. What do you think, Mr. Rolling?"

"It would take a good swimmer to go clear under her broad beam," I answered. "I don't believe there's any one aboard who could do it, even with a line around him."

England, the stout sailor, was standing near the rail while I spoke.

"If ye don't mind, sir, I'll try me hand at it. Put a line about me body to haul me in if a shark takes a notion to make a run fer me. Don't haul unless ye have to, mind, or ye'll scrape the hide off me body."

"Go ahead at it," said Sackett.

The heavy man slipped off his jumper in a moment, and I noticed the huge muscles of his chest and arms. He must have made a good prize fighter in his day. Coming out on the frame, he had the line stopped around his waist and then started at the fore rigging to go under the ship to the other side.

Nearly all hands came to the rail to watch him, although the water was knee deep on the deck at this point. He dived gracefully under the side, and as the bubbles disappeared I could see him going like a fish beneath the shimmering copper, which gave forth a greenish light in the sunshine. The line was payed out fast, and in a few moments he arose to port none the worse for the trip.

Nothing came of this, as he was too much taken up with the endeavor to go clear to see anything. His next trip was a fathom or so further aft, and this time he saw nothing save a very foul bottom. After taking a rest and a nip of grog he started again, going more slowly as he gained confidence.

Six trips tired him greatly in spite of his strength, and he sat for some minutes upon the frame before making his plunge. Then he stood up and dived again.

I could see him swimming down, down, down under the ship's bilge, growing to a faint brownish yellow speck which wavered and shook with the refraction of the disturbed surface. Then while I looked the line slacked, and the brownish yellow object beneath wavered into a larger size. Evidently he was coming up and had failed to make the five fathoms necessary to go clear of the keel. I hauled in the line rapidly, for I knew that he must be exhausted to give it up so soon. The wavering brown spot grew quickly in size, and in a moment, outlined upon it, I made out the figure of England straining away for the surface. I hauled frantically to aid him, and the next moment he broke water and was landed upon the frame, while the great brown object beneath rose right behind him, and took the form of a tremendous hammer-headed shark. It came up in an instant and broached clear of the water at least three feet, but failed to reach the frame where Bull England clung panting and gasping for breath.

"I reckon I've had me dose this time," said he, between his gasps; "I almost swam down the feller's throat. I ain't exactly skeered, but I'm too tired to try agin this afternoon, so if any one wants me place on the end o' this line, he can take it while I rests."

"Faith," said Chips, "if ye ain't skeered ye'll be so fast enough if ye go in agin. Look at th' monster! Did ye iver see sech a head? Wan would think he had sense enough not to be eatin' av a tough sailorman. Big head, nothin' in it, as the sayin' is."

Andrews was standing near the rail and appeared much interested in the diver's work. The fact that it had been interrupted angered him. His face took on that hideous expression of ferocity I knew meant mischief, and a string of the foulest oaths followed. He drew forth his pistol and raised it slowly to a line with his eye on the shark's head, now just awash under the frame a few feet distant.

"Crack!"

The bullet struck it fair on the crown where it was fully three feet across the eyes. It smashed through, and the huge fish sank slowly under the force of the stroke.

Then it suddenly recovered itself and tore the water into foam, lashing out with its tail and turning over and over, snapping with its great jaws.

"It is an unnecessary cruelty, Mr. Andrews," said Sackett, loudly. "Put that weapon up. It is no use to kill to satisfy a murderous heart. The fish would leave us in a few moments if it were fed."

"Watch the Lord's anointed feed it then," snarled the ruffian, with a fierce oath. "Say a pater for its soul, for it's on its way to hell."

With that he fired again as the fish broached clear, and I must say one could hardly help admiring his shooting. The heavy bullet struck within an inch of the first, although the mark was now several fathoms distant and thrashing about at a great rate.

The shark whirled round and started off, leaving a trail of blood which showed like a dark cloud in its wake. In a moment it had disappeared.

"Don't swear so hard, my dear Mr. Andrews," cried Mr. Bell, in his high, piping voice. "You'll scare all the fish."

Andrews coolly broke his pistol at the breech and tossed out the empty shells. Then he reloaded it and handed it to the smiling, rosy-cheeked third mate.

"You stand by and take care of things while I spell Bull England a bit," said he. "Journegan," he continued, calling to the English mate, "you take the line for a while, and let that young fellow rest, while I try her bilge aft."

He stripped off his shirt and stood in his trousers. When I saw him, I no longer wondered why I had failed to overcome him in our first set-to. The fellow was a perfect mass of muscle, and while I gazed at his strong frame I wondered at the power in Trunnell's arms, which held us so tight and saved me that first day on board.

He came out on the frame, and I made way for Journegan to take the line. He took a turn, and over he went without delay.

After four or five attempts to get under the ship, he finally came to the surface with news. He had been under her bilge, clear down to the keel on a line with the main channels. Not being able to get further, and seeing the dark shadow of the keel ahead, he made out to examine as far as he could go. Close to her garboard strake on the starboard side he saw where a large butt had started, owing probably to the bad loading of the ship. This plank end starting outboard was evidently where the water came in.

Andrews came on deck after this, and all hands began overhauling gear to get a mattress upon the hole. Lines were rove and passed under the ship's bilge and keel. These were made fast on deck to the stump of the mizzen mast, and their ends brought to the capstan through snatch blocks. Planks were then strapped loosely on the lines and allowed to run along them freely, being weighted sufficiently to cause them to sink. After they were slung clear of the ship, they were held in position until a pad of canvas and oakum was inserted between them and the side.

It was quite late in the evening before this was accomplished, and work had to be stopped until daylight.

At the evening meal Andrews was more sulky than usual. It appeared that now, since there was a chance of stopping the leak, we would all be aboard the ship when she made port, for with the water out of her we might easily make the Cape in a fortnight.

Sackett said grace as usual, standing up and bowing gravely over the long board.

"What's the sense of asking the Lord to make us truly thankful for stuff what ain't fit to eat anyway," growled Andrews, when he finished. "You ain't got nothin' to be so blamed thankful for, captain. This grub'll sure make some of the men sick before we're through. If I ain't mistaken, some of them will be down with trouble before the leak is swabbed."

"I'll say what I think best, sir, at my table. If you don't like it, you can eat with the men," answered Sackett.

"Oh, I never said nothin' to the contrary, did I?" asked the fellow.

"Well, pay a little more attention to your behavior, or I'll make a passenger of you on board," said Sackett, who had lost patience.

"I never came here on those conditions, and I fail to accept them, my Lord's anointed. I wasn't asked to come aboard here. Since I'm here, I'll have my rights, and I don't call to mind the names of any one around about this ship as will take it upon theirselves to start an argument to the contrary. No, sir, I'll obey orders so long as they're sensible, but don't try to run it on a man like me, Sackett. I ain't the sort of stuff you're made to run against."

"Oh, Captain Andrews, you have such a dreadful way with you," piped Bell, the third mate, in his high voice. "Don't you know you really frightened me with such strong words."

Journegan laughed outright.

"If I have to put up with any more of your insolence, sir," said Sackett, quietly, "I'll have you bound and put away until we are in port."

"Oh, please don't hurt me, captain," cried Andrews, with his ugly smile. "I ain't going to do nothing mutinous."

"Well, stop talking to me, sir. Every word you say is mutinous. I'll have silence at this table, sir, if I have to bind you up."

"Cruel, unchristian man!" cried Andrews. "Journegan, my boy, this shows the uselessness of prayer. Here's a man praying one minute, and before the Lord has time to answer him he's ready to commit murder. Sink me, if ever I did see any use of praying one minute and doing things the next. It's wrorse than my pore old father used to be. 'My son,' he'd say, 'shake out the bunt of yer breeches,' which I'd do. Yessir, sink me if I didn't do it. 'Shake out the bunt of yer breeches and come here.' Then he'd grab me and yank me acrost his knee. 'Lord guide a righteous hand,' he'd say, and with that down would come that righteous hand like the roof of a house where the bunt of my pants had been. 'Lord give me strength to lead him into the straight and narrow path,' he'd whine; and sink me, Journegan, if he wouldn't give me a twist that would slew my innerds askew and send me flying acrost the room. Lead me into the straight and narrow path? Man alive, he'd send me drifting along that path like a bullet from a gun. What's the sense of it, hey?"

"There ain't none," said Journegan, snickering and rubbing his whiskers in appreciation of his friend's wit.

"Mr. Journegan," said Sackett, "you go on deck, sir."

"What am I doing?" asked the fellow, with a smirk.

"You go on deck, sir, or I'll be forced to take some action in the matter of discipline. Do you understand?" continued Sackett, now red in the face with anger.

Journegan rose leisurely from the table and went up the companion, whistling.

"And now, my young man," continued Sackett, addressing the third mate, "I don't want to have to tie you up with your friend, but you are not one of my crew, and I'll trouble you to keep still at my table. Mr. Andrews," he went on, "you'll have no further authority aboard here, and the sooner you get into the boat with the rest, the better it will be for you."

"That's where you make a mistake," said Andrews, coolly. "I'm second in command here now, and I'll stay until the ship sinks or goes to port, in spite of you or any one else, unless you care to give me credit for my share of salvage as a volunteer to bring her in."

"You will go to your room and not take any further part in the management of the vessel, I say," Captain Sackett ordered, "If you don't go freely, I'll order my men to assist you."

"If there's any one who cares to take the responsibility, let him step out and make known his name," said Andrews, in an even tone.

Sackett left the table and went on deck at once. I heard him calling for Jenks, England, and the rest, and I started up the companion, thinking to take a hand with Chips and Jim and our men. As I did so, Andrews cursed me foully, and the third mate made a remark I failed to hear.

Meeting Chips and Johnson, I sent the latter for Jim and Hans. Phillippi stood near the wheel, and I beckoned to him. When the six of us were together, I told them in a few words that Sackett was going to tie Andrews up for mutiny. They would stand by me and give him help if necessary.

We waited near the edge of the poop while Sackett told his men what he wanted done with Andrews.

"Men," said he, "there's only one captain aboard here, and that is myself. If you disobey me, it is mutiny, and you know the penalty."

"It ain't that we're scared of him," said England, "but he's a tough one to take without no weapons."

"I don't ask you to run any risk," said Sackett. "I'll take him and give him to you to tie up and keep until we're safe in port. You must do this or you will be insubordinate."

"Sure," said Dog Daniels, "if you'll take the fellow, we'll guarantee to keep him fast enough. Hey, Jenks, ain't that so?"

I thought I saw a suspicion of a smile play over the old sailor's wrinkled face, and the seams of his leather-like jaws seemed to grow deeper.

"That's it," said Dalton. "You take him, and we'll take care of him until you say let him loose."

Journegan was at the wheel with one of the men who had left with the old sailor, Jenks. Sackett did not question him in regard to the matter of Andrews, as he evidently thought he had already showed signs of mutiny.

"I'm sorry to have this trouble aboard, sir," said Sackett to me, as he turned to go down the companion to the cabin. "You and your men can stand aside while this matter is arranged satisfactorily. Afterward you will have to take your man away with you when you can go."

"I'm very sorry the thing has occurred as it has, captain," I said. "We'll stand by you, if you wish, and help you to carry out any orders."

"I don't think it will be necessary," answered Sackett. "However, if anything disagreeable happens, I trust you will do what you may for the welfare of my daughter, sir. You understand how much she is at the mercy of these ruffians, should anything happen to me."

"I will pass my word, sir," I answered. "Your daughter shall come to no harm while there are a few American sailors afloat to do anything. I do warn you, though, to keep a lookout on that ruffian. He has tried to take my life twice, and is under sentence for a murder. Don't let him get his gun out at you, or there might be an accident."

"A nice fellow for your captain to send me," said Sackett. "It was no fault of yours, my friend, so don't think I blame you," he added hastily.

He started toward the companionway, and had just reached it alone when the grizzled head of Andrews appeared above the combings. The fellow stood forth on deck and was followed by our third mate.

"Lay aft, here, England and Daniels," cried Sackett.

The men came slowly along the poop. Jenks and Dalton, followed by six others of the *Sovereign's* crew who had chosen to desert the ship, walked aft to the quarter to see if there was anything for them to do. Some of these men were true to their captain without doubt; but Jenks placed himself in their front, and by the strange smile the old sailor had, I knew he was looking for trouble.

Sackett went straight up to Andrews and stood before him, and for one brief moment the tableau presented was dramatic enough to be impressed forcibly upon my memory. It was sturdy, honest manhood against lawlessness and mutiny. A brave, kind-hearted, religious man, alone, against the worst human devil I have ever seen or heard of. He was, indeed, a desperate ruffian, whose life was already forfeited, but Sackett never flinched for a moment.

XV

The dull night of the southern ocean was closing around the scene on the *Sovereign's* deck, making the faces of the men indistinct in the gloom. The Englishmen stood a little apart from ours, but all looked at the captain as he walked up to Andrews. England and Daniels stopped when they were within a fathom of their skipper as though awaiting further orders before proceeding with their unpleasant duty.

The mutineer turned slowly at Sackett's approach as though disdaining to show haste in defence. Then, as the stout, bearded commander halted in front of him, he raised his head and gave forth that snort of contempt and annoyance which I knew to mean mischief.

"Captain Andrews," said Sackett, "you will turn over your weapons to me, sir. I don't allow my officers to carry them aboard this ship. Afterward I shall have to place you in arrest until you see fit to obey orders and show proper discipline, sir."

"Now see here, my old fellow," said Andrews, "I don't want to hurt you, but I've obeyed orders here and will obey them when they don't relate to what I shall eat or say at the table. Don't try any of your infernal monkey games on me, or you might get hurt."

"Will you hand over your weapon, sir?" said Sackett, advancing, and standing close before him.

Andrews pulled out his long revolver and pointed it at the skipper's head. Then he gave a snort of anger and glared savagely at the Englishman.

Sackett turned to his men.

"Seize him, and disarm him," he ordered. But England and Daniels stood motionless. Journegan stepped to one side to keep out of the line of fire.

Sackett made a move forward, as if to seize the weapon. There was a sharp explosion, and both men disappeared for an instant in the spurt of smoke. Then I saw Sackett stagger sidelong across the deck with the roll of the ship, and go down heavily upon the wheel gratings. He uttered no word. I ran to his side, and saw the ashy hue coming upon his ruddy face, and knew his time was short. I heard the uproar of voices that followed the moment of silence after the shot, but took no heed. Placing my hand under his head, I called for Jim to get some brandy from below. Then I bawled for Chips and the rest to seize the murderer.

Sackett turned up his kind eyes to mine, and whispered: "I'll be dead in a few minutes, Mr. Rolling. Do what you can for my men. I tried to do my duty, sir, and I expect every honest man to do his. Save my—"

The light had gone out. He was limp and dead on the deck of the ship he had tried so nobly to save. My hand was wet with blood, and as I withdrew it, the wild abhorrence of the thing came upon me.

I stood up, and there, within ten feet of me, was that sneering ruffian standing coolly, with his pistol in his hand.

It was such a cold-blooded, horrible thing, done without warning, that I was speechless. Chips stood near my side, cursing softly, and looking with fierce eyes at the assassin. Jim came up the companionway, but saw that all was over. My three sailors were like statues, Phillippi muttering unintelligibly.

For nearly a minute after the thing happened I stood there gazing at Andrews and the rest, paralyzed for action, but noting each and every movement of the men as though some movement on their part would give me a cue how to act.

All of a sudden the piping voice of our third mate rose in a laugh, while he cried, "He's gone to heaven."

It was as though something gave away within me, and before I fairly knew what I was doing, I was rushing upon Andrews to close.

I remember seeing a bright flash and feeling a heavy blow on my left side. Then I found myself in the scuppers looking up at a struggle upon the *Sovereign's* quarter-deck.

At the signal of my rush for Andrews, Jim, who was somewhat expert at tackling persons, dashed at him also from starboard. Chips instantly followed on the other side, and then, our men seeing how things were to go, closed from the rear. All six of us would have met at Andrews as a converging point, had it not been for the scoundrel's pistol.

His first shot struck me fairly under the heart. It knocked me over, and I rolled to port, deathly sick. Thinking for a moment I was killed, I made no immediate effort to recover myself, but lay vomiting and clutching my side. Then in a moment the weakness began to leave me, and I was aware that I was clutching the heavy knife I carried in my breast pocket. I drew it forth, and as I did so, something fell to the deck at my side, and I saw it was a piece of lead. Then I saw that Andrews's bullet had jammed itself into the joint of the hilt, smashing flat on the steel and breaking up, part of it falling away as I drew it forth. The knife had saved my life; for the shot had been true, and would have been instantly fatal had it penetrated.

I started to my feet and saw Jim lying motionless just outside the swaying crowd, which had now closed about the murderer. At that instant Andrews fired again, and Hans, who had tried to use his knife, staggered out of the group and fell dead. Three of the *Sovereign's* own men who had intended going back with us were now in the fracas also, and as I started in two more joined.

I saw Phillippi's knife flash for an instant. Then came a fierce oath from Andrews, followed by a snort of rage and pain. Another shot followed instantly, and Phillippi was lying outside the swaying figures with a bloody hole through his forehead.

The only thing I remember as I forced my way into the group and struck at the scoundrel was that he had one more shot, and I wondered if he would land it before we had him.

He warded off my knife-stroke by a desperate wrench, but the blade ripped his right arm to the bone from shoulder to elbow, laming it absolutely. Even as it was, he lowered his weapon and fired it instantly as it was seized. An Englishman named Williams was struck through the body and lived but a moment afterward. Chips now had the weapon by the barrel, and just as I was about to drive my knife into the murderer over the shoulder of Johnson, a heavy hand seized my collar and I was dragged back. Wrenching myself around, I found that I was engaging the tall sailor, Daniels, and as I did so, Journegan, England, Dalton, Jenks, and our third officer fell upon the crowd which had borne Andrews to the deck.

All of the English sailors who had started to leave the *Sovereign* were now fighting with Chips, Johnson, and myself, making eight men as against six. But the six were of the strongest and most determined rascals that ever trod a ship's deck.

As every sailor carries a sheath-knife, the fight promised to be an interesting one if the men of the *Sovereign's* crew saw fit to fight it out. England, however, who was stronger than any two of our men, did not like going into the matter with the same spirit as Journegan, Daniels, and Andrews. After he had received a severe cut and had cracked the skull of the sailor who had given it by knocking him over the head with an iron belaying-pin, he began to retreat along the deck. Chips had planted his knife in Andrews's thigh, and had cut Dalton and Journegan badly in the mix-up.

The Irishman was unharmed save for a few scratches, and being aided by Johnson, he soon had the men backing away toward the break of the poop, the third mate crying out shrilly to stop fighting. The queer young man was defending Andrews mightily with a knife, and for this reason alone the scoundrel managed to get to his feet and retreat with the rest, backing away as they did to the mizzen and from there to the poop rail, where they were brought to bay.

Daniels, however, fared worse. We had a struggle for some moments alone, and just as my knife was in a good position a man struck him from behind, throwing him off his guard and letting my blade penetrate his throat until it protruded three inches beyond the back of his neck. Then the fight was over.

Chips stopped at my side with Andrews's revolver in his hand.

"'Tis a pity we've no cartridges fer th' weepin," he panted; "'twould save th' hangman a lot o' trouble. Now there'll be a butcher's shop aboard."

"Come on," I said. "You get to starboard, and I'll take the port side. We'll rush them and make a finish of it. Here, Frank," I called to a sailor, "lend me your knife. Mine's no good for this work."

"My own is broken, sir," said he.

"Hold on," cried Journegan; "we're not making any fight."

I could see the five ruffians talking brokenly together while they recovered their breath. Our third mate was holding forth in a piping tone, but too low for me to hear the words.

"We don't want to press the outfly any further," said England. "We ain't no pirates. All we did was to defend ourselves. One of your fellows cut me arm open and I hit him over the head, not meanin' no more than to knock him out for the time bein', as the sayin' is."

"Will you surrender and put down your knives?" I asked.

Andrews gave his fierce snort and was about to say something in reply, but the third mate seized him and stopped him. The assassin was badly wounded and swayed as he stood, but his spirit was not in the least beaten. He had killed five men out of six shots from his pistol and would have had me in the list but for the knife I placed in my breast as a precaution at the warning from Chips on taking him aboard. His coolness and steadiness were marvellous. Not a shot had he wasted, and if he had been relieved a trifle sooner by his half-hearted followers, he would have had the whole crowd of us at his mercy. No man could have faced a pistol of that size in the hands of one so quick and steady.

There was no answer to my question, and I repeated it, Chips adding that they would go free if they would give up the men who had done killing.

"Why o' course, we ain't no pirates," said Journegan.

"Well, chuck out your knives, or we'll be for closing with you," I cried. "This thing is over, and one or the other will be in command."

"Why don't ye take the boat an' go clear? Dalton, here, will give ye the provisions, an' you can get to the north'ard and make port. There ain't no room for both of us aboard here now, even if we gave up, which we ain't got no idea o' doin' unless you come out square an' fair."

"Yes," said Jenks, "you men don't want to make a Kilkenny cat go out of this ship. Do the square an' fair thing, an' git out. You know, Tommy," he went on, addressing a sailor, "I don't want to hurt you; but you know me. You boys can't make no show agin an old man-o'-war's man like me, as has been up to his waist in blood many a time, an' never ware the worse for it."

The sailor addressed spoke to me.

"Don't you think it a good way, sir? They are good for us if they try hard, for England can whip any three of us, an' I, for one, don't want to run against him if it can be helped. We have a boat."

"Nonsense," said Chips. "We must take 'em."

I thought a moment. There was a young girl below. Probably she was even now frightened nearly to death. If anything did go wrong with us,—and it certainly looked as if it would, when I sized up that crowd,—she would be worse than dead. There were seven of us left against six, although Andrews was too badly hurt to fear, but they were much better men physically. After they had once started to do for us, they were not the kind who would stick at anything. I was much exhausted, myself, and while I thought the matter over, it seemed as though to go were the better way out of the trouble.

Chips, however, insisted on closing with the men.

It took me some minutes to convince him that the young fellows with us were not of the kind to depend on in such a fracas, and that he would be in a bad way should he tackle England alone. Journegan, Jenks, and Dalton were all powerful men, armed with sheath-knives sharper and better than our own, for they had evidently prepared for just such an emergency.

"Let Dalton provision the whale-boat, and you men get out," said Mr. Bell after I had finished whispering my views to Chips.

"Yes," said the steward; "you men stay where you are, and I'll put the stuff aboard for you, and then you can get out."

"All right," I answered; "go ahead."

Some of us sat about the after-skylight, while Andrews and his gang disposed themselves, as comfortably as they might, around the mizzen. Dalton went down over the poop, and entered the cabin from forward, and Chips, Johnson, and myself looked over our dead.

Jim lay where he fell. There was no sign of life, and Chips swore softly at the villain's work, when we laid his head back upon the planks. Hans breathed slightly, but he was going fast. We poured some spirits between his lips, but he relaxed, and was lifeless in a few minutes. Phillippi lay with his eyes staring up at the sky. His knife was still clutched in his dark hand, and his teeth shone white beneath his black mustache. The other sailor was dead, and while we looked for some sign of life, I heard a smothered sob come from aft. We turned and saw a slender white form bending over the body of Captain Sackett. The moon was rising in the east, lighting the heavens and making a long silver wake over the calm ocean. By its light I made out Miss Sackett, holding the head of her dead father in her lap, and crying softly.

XVI

The moon rose higher, and Dalton came and went, carrying provisions up from the cabin. These he lowered into our boat, which was hauled alongside, Jenks taking a hand when necessary, although he never came aft far enough to encounter any of our men. Andrews sat quietly on the deck and had his cuts bound up and dressed, while Mr. Bell went below to the medicine chest for whatever he wanted. We kept well apart, each side feeling a distrust for the other, and neither caring to provoke a conflict.

In about an hour Dalton announced the boat was ready.

"There's salt junk enough for all hands a week or two, and ship's bread for a month. There's water in the breaker. You can go when you're ready," said Journegan.

I went aft to Miss Sackett, where she had sat motionless for a long time with her face buried in her hands, as if to shut out the cruel sight around her.

"We will leave the ship in a few minutes," said I, taking her by the hand, and trying to raise her gently to her feet. "You must try to bear up to go with us. Try to walk evenly and quickly when the time comes, for there may be a struggle yet."

She let fall her hands from her face, and I saw her eyes, dry and bright in the moonlight.

"Can't you kill them?" she asked quietly. "Oh, if I were only a man!" Then she drew herself up to her full height, and gazed hard at the group of ruffians at the mizzen.

"I'll have to go below first, and get my things," she said. "I suppose you know what is best, to go or stay?"

"Hurry," I said. "I will wait here at the companion."

She went below with a firm tread, and I heard her slam the door of her stateroom. Andrews looked toward me and spoke.

"You can leave the girl aboard," said he. "You'll have enough in the boat."

"Chips," I called, "stand by for a rush. Don't let Dalton get forward alive. Miss Sackett either goes with us, or we all stay here together and fight it out."

Andrews, who had recovered somewhat, now staggered to his feet and drew his knife.

"Stand by and follow along the port rail," he said to Journegan and England. "You two," addressing Bell and Jenks, "go to starboard."

Dalton, who was below and separated from his fellows, would be our object.

Jenks, however, remonstrated at the attack.

"Hold on," said he, and England stopped. "What's the use of crowding in this thing like this? Some of us will get killed sure with seven fresh men out for it, and what's the use? All for a gal. No, sir, says I, don't go making a fool job of the thing. I ain't out for murder, not fer no gal."

"You'll do as I say or get done," answered Andrews, with a fierce snort, turning toward him.

Jenks backed toward us, and Bell tried to hold Andrews back. He partly succeeded, but was close enough to the old man-o'-war's man to get a slight cut from a blow meant for Andrews. Then England took a hand, and with Journegan they held the assassin in check.

Jenks came toward us.

"I'll go with you fellows if you say so," said he, and he tossed his knife over the rail to show that he meant no treachery.

"'Tis a little late ye are, but ye're welcome," said Chips, who had advanced at my cry nearly to him. Frank, the young English sailor, and Johnson were both close behind Chins, with the rest following. It looked as if there would be a collision, after all.

"Take the girl and go," screamed Bell, almost fainting from the cut received.

"Yes, take her and be damned!" cried Journegan. "Only get off before it's too late."

"Seems to me," said Chips, "we could do for them now wid no trouble. Let's try 'em."

Johnson advanced at the word, but I called him back just as Chips was making ready for a spring at England. The big prize fighter had made ready for the Irishman, and for an instant it seemed that we would have another ending of the affair.

"Come," I said to one of the young sailors who held back, "get aboard the small boat," and the fellow, who was shrinking from the knives, took the opportunity to get away. This made Chips hesitate, and in another moment I had two more of the men going over the side.

Miss Sackett came on deck. Her face was ruddy even in the moonlight, but she carried herself with a firm step to the mizzen channels.

"Stand by and hold her below there," I bawled, and a man received her into the boat. Then I called to the rest of our fellows and threw a leg over the rail to signify that we were going. They came along, Chips last, with Johnson at his side. The carpenter was furious and wanted to fight it out, and it would have taken very little to have set him upon them alone. They, however, when Andrews had been overcome, were by no means anxious to engage. This seemed strange to me, for they certainly were men who feared nothing, and the sooner we were out of the way, the surer they were of getting safe off with their necks. Just what made Bell so determined to have us go was a puzzle to me. As Chips climbed over the rail, England came to the side with Journegan. I expected some outburst, and for an instant the carpenter was at a disadvantage. But they let him go over without a hostile movement. He stood up in the bow while a man shoved off.

"Ah, ye raskils, it's like runnin' away we are, but we ain't. It's but lavin' to th' hangman what I'd do meself, curse ye."

The boat of the *Sovereign* towing at the quarter came abreast us as we dropped back. Chips still standing and glaring at the ship, with rage in his voice and eyes.

He stooped down and lifted an oar as the small boat came alongside, and with a half-suppressed yell smote her with all his strength upon the gunwale. The oar crashed through nearly to the water line under the power of the stroke.

"Blast ye," he cried, "ye'll niver leave that ship alive," and he smote the boat again and again, crushing her down until she began to fill. Johnson took a hand also in spite of England and Journegan hauling away at the painter. Our men backed water so hard they held her back until the boat was hopelessly stove and had settled to the thwarts. Then we let go and drifted away, while the men aboard the *Sovereign* hurled belaying-pins and gratings at us.

"A pleasant voyage to you," came the soft notes of Mr. Bell's voice; and then we rowed slowly away to the northward, leaving the *Sovereign* a dark, sunken grisly thing against the moonlit sky.

"Rig the mast and sail," I said. "It's no use getting tired before the struggle comes. We're some six hundred miles out, and may not raise a vessel for days."

The oars were taken in, and the tarpaulin which had done duty for a sail was rigged. Under the pressure of the light air the whale-boat made steering-way and a little more. The moon now made the night as light as day, and although it was slightly chilly in this latitude, we suffered little from the exposure, each settling himself into the most comfortable position possible, and gazing back at the strange black outline of the wrecked ship. Her sunken decks and patched-up jury rig with the trysail set from the after-stay gave her an uncanny look, while her masts and spars with the set canvas seemed as black as ink against the light sky beyond. There she lay, a horrid, ghastly thing, wallowing along slowly toward a port she would never reach.

While I looked at her, Miss Sackett burst into a hard laugh which jangled hysterically. She had been silent since she had entered the boat, and this sudden burst startled me. Her eyes were fixed upon the grim derelict. They shone in the moonlight and she choked convulsively.

"Can I hand you some water, ma'm?" asked Jenks.

"What made you come with us, you rogue?" she asked, without turning her head.

"I was with ye from the start, s'help me," said Jenks. "I only goes with the other side when I feared they'd kill all hands."

"Well, it's a good thing for you, you contemptible rascal," she answered in an even tone.

All of a sudden I noticed a flicker of light above the cabin of the *Sovereign*. It died away for an instant and then flared again, Miss Sackett laughed convulsively.

"Look," she said.

At that instant a red glare flashed up from the derelict. It shone on her maintopsail and staysails and lit up the ocean around her.

"Faith, but she's afire," cried Chips. "Look at them."

I turned the boat's head around and ran her off before the wind, hauling up again and standing for the wreck to get near her. Miss Sackett seized my arm and held it fast.

"Don't go back for them!" she cried. "You shall not go back for them!"

"I haven't the least intention of going for them," I answered; "I only wanted to get close enough to see what they'd do. Did you set her afire?" I asked bluntly.

"Of course I did," said the girl, passionately. "Do you suppose I didn't hear them telling you I should have to remain aboard? What else was there left for me to do? Would you have me fall into their hands?"

"Lord save ye, but ye did the right thing," said Chips. Johnson echoed this sentiment.

"An' I knew ye ware up to somethin' of the kind when ye went below," said Jenks, "fer I smelled the smoke and thought to stop it, but there ware too much risk as it was to add fire, so I had to step out o' the crowd an' jine ye. I never did nothin' in the fracas, as ye know, except get hurt."

In ten minutes we were close aboard the derelict, and her cabin was a mass of flame. Figures of men showed against the light amidships, and I finally made out all hands getting out a spar and barrels to make a raft. The oil in the cargo, however, was too quick for them. It had become ignited aft and had cut off all retreat by the stove-in boat. Several explosions followed, and the flames roared high above the maintopsail. Journegan, Andrews, and another man were seen making their way forward across the sunken deck. The heat drove them to the topgallant forecastle and in a few minutes we could see all standing there near the windlass. The bitts sheltered them from the heat.

The oil in the ship was not submerged in the after part, owing to her trimming by the head. It had been the last stuff put aboard and was well up under her cabin deck. Even that which was awash caught after the fire had started to heat things up well, and the entire after part of the *Sovereign* was a mass of flames. They gave forth a brilliant light, glowing red and making the sky appear dark beyond. Great clouds of sparks from the woodwork above soared into the heavens. The light must have been visible for miles.

There was absolutely no escape for the men aboard now, except by getting away on some float. Journegan, Dalton, and England were working hard at something on the forecastle which appeared to be a raft. The one they had started aft they had been forced to abandon after an explosion. The carpenter's tools being below in the hold when the ship filled, they had nothing but their knives and a small hatchet left to work with.

Suddenly Mr. Bell made us out in the darkness less than a quarter of a mile distant. He screamed for us to come back and take him off the derelict.

"Pay no attention to him," said Chips.

I hesitated, with the tiller in my hand. The end of those men seemed so horrible that I forgot for the instant what they had done.

"You shall not go back for them while I'm aboard this boat," said Miss Sackett, quietly, from her seat beside me, and she seized the tiller firmly to luff the craft.

"I didn't intend to," I answered; "yet that man's cry had so much of the woman in it that it was instinctive to turn."

"Instinctive or not, here we stay. He is the biggest devil of the lot," answered the girl. "There's some horrible game in getting us away. I'm certain of it, but don't know what it can be. We'll find out when it's too late."

"We might take them aboard one at a time and bind them," I suggested. This was greeted with growlings from Chips and Johnson. Even Jenks declared it would never do, and the other sailors made antagonistic remarks. There was nothing to do but keep away and let them save themselves as best they might.

We sailed slowly around the wreck, watching her burn. Hour after hour she flamed and hissed, the heat being felt at a hundred fathoms distant. And all the while, the sharp, piping voice of our third mate screamed shrilly for succor.

After midnight the *Sovereign* had burned clear to the water line from aft to amidships. Even her rails along the waist were burning fiercely with the oil that had been thrown upon them by the explosions of the heated barrels. And as she burned out her oil, she sank lower and lower in the water until she gave forth huge clouds of steam and smoke instead of flaring flames. In the early hours of the morning, we were still within two hundred fathoms of her; and she showed nothing in the gray light save the mainmast and the topgallant forecastle. Her canvas had gone, and the bare black pole of her mast stuck out of the sea, which now flowed deep around the foot of it. Upon the blackened forecastle head, five human forms crouched behind the sheltering bulk of the windlass. They were silent now and motionless. While I looked, one of them staggered to his feet and stretched out his hands above his head, gazing at the light in the east. It was Andrews. He raised his clenched fists and shook them fiercely at us and at the gray sky above. Then over the calm, silent ocean came the fierce, raving curses of the doomed villain.

A gentle air was stirring the swell in the east, which soon filled our sail. We kept the boat's head away until she pointed in the direction of the African cape. And so we sailed away, with the echoes of that villain's voice ringing in our ears, calling forth fierce curses upon the God he had denied.

I turned away from the horrible spectacle of that grisly hulk with its human burden. As I did so, my eyes met those of Miss Sackett. She lowered hers, took out her handkerchief and, bowing over, buried her face in it, crying as though her heart would break.

XVII

"If you'll pass the pannikin, I'll take a drink, sir," said Jenks, after the sun had risen and warmed the chilly air of the southern ocean.

I tossed the old man-o'-war's man the measure, and he proceeded to draw a cupful from the water breaker, which was full and lay amidships.

"It's an uncommon quare taste the stuff has, sure enough," said he, after he had laid aside his quid and drank a mouthful, "Try a bit, Tom," he went on, and passed the pannikin to a sailor next him.

"You're always lookin' fer trouble, old man," said the sailor, draining off the cupful.

"An' bloomin' well ready to get out of it by any way he can," added another. "Fill her up agin an' let me have some. This sun is most hot, in spite of the breeze. Blast me, Jenks, but you're a suspicious one. It's a wonder you ever go to sleep."

The young sailor, Tom, put down the cup and watched Jenks draw it full again. Then he grew pale.

"Hold on a bit with that water, you men. There's something wrong with it," he said. He gulped and placed his hand over his abdomen, while a spasm of pain passed over his features.

"My God!" he muttered, and doubled up. Then he vomited violently and his spasms increased.

I saw Chips turn white under his tan, and Johnson look with staring eyes at the water breaker, as though it were a ghost.

"Knock in the head," I said, "and let's see what's inside of it."

Two men held the poor fellow gasping over the rail while his agony grew worse. The rest crowded around aft as much as possible to see what terrible fate was in store for us.

The breaker was upended in a moment. Jenks stove in the head with an oar handle, and we peered inside.

The water was a clear crystal, like that in the *Sovereign's* tanks. It was not discolored in the least.

"Pass the bailer here," I said; "and then turn the barrel so we can get the sunlight into it."

I bailed out a few quarts, looked at it carefully, tasted it slightly, and then put it carefully back again I noticed a strange acrid taste. The barrel was turned toward the sun, and its light was allowed to shine straight into its depths. I put my head down close to the surface and peered hard at the bottom. Then I was aware of a whitish powder which showed against the dark wood. Reaching down, some of this was brought up; and then I recognized the same powder Captain Sackett had told me was bichloride of mercury.

By this time Tom was in convulsions. He strained horribly, and we could do nothing to relieve his agony. Brandy was given, but it did no good, and finally he lost consciousness. Miss Sackett nursed him tenderly and did all she could to make him comfortable, but it was no use.

The horror of the thing fairly took my senses for a moment. There we were, miles away from land, without water. The villains had meant us to tell no tales. All adrift in an open boat, with food and water poisoned, we had a small chance indeed of ever telling the story of the *Sovereign's* loss. Vessels were not plentiful at the high latitude we were in; and, as we were out of the trade, it was doubtful if we could even get into the track of the regular Cape route inside a week, to say nothing of being picked up. It seemed as though Andrews' villany would finish us yet.

Far away on the southern horizon, the single mast stuck up above the blue water like a black rod. I stood up and gazed at it. Chips appeared to read my thoughts, for he spoke out:—

"'Tis no use now, sir; the tanks would be a couple o' fathoms deep, an' we couldn't get at them. She won't float more'n a day or two, anyhow, wid th' afterdeck an' cargo burnt free. She'll go under as soon as the oil's washed out wid a sea, and that'll be th' last av a bad ship."

I saw that the carpenter was right. There was no water for either Andrews or ourselves, and it would be foolish to go back to force the tank.

"Heave the stuff overboard," I said, and Johnson and Jenks raised the barrel upon the rail. It poured out clear into the blue ocean, and showed no sign of its deadly character.

"Break out that barrel of ship's bread," said Chips.

It was found to be moistened with water all through, and as even the little poison I had drunk made me horribly nauseated, there was no thought of tasting the stuff. Over the side it went, floating high in the boat's wake. Then came the beef.

"Hold on with that," said Miss Sackett. "It isn't likely they'd poison everything. I don't remember there being over several pounds of that mercury in the medicine chest, and you know it won't dissolve readily in water. They must have had something to dissolve it in first, and it would have taken too long to fill everything full of the stuff."

"Who cares to taste the beef?" I asked.

"Give me a piece, sir," said Johnson.

He put it in his mouth and chewed slowly upon it at first, as though not quite certain whether to swallow it or not. Finally he mustered courage and made away with a portion of it, waiting some minutes to see if it produced pain. It was apparently all right, and then he swallowed the rest. We concluded to keep the beef and eat it as a last resort.

The breeze freshened in the southeast, and we ran along steadily. If it held, we could make about a hundred miles a day, and raise the African coast within a week. There was a chance, if we could stand the strain.

It was now the sixth day since we had left the *Pirate*, and we figured that she must have rounded the Cape, and would now be standing along up the South Atlantic with the steady southeast trade behind her. Other ships would be in the latitude of Cape Town, and if we could make the northing, we might raise one and be picked up. I pictured the horrors the poor girl sitting beside me must endure if we were adrift for days in the whale-boat. What she had already gone through was enough to shake the nerves of the strongest woman, but here she sat, quietly looking at the water, her eyes sometimes filled with tears, while not a word of complaint escaped her lips.

Her example nerved me. I had passed the order to stop all talking except when necessary, as it would only add to thirst. We ran along in silence.

We had no compass save the one hanging to my watch-chain, as big as my thumb-nail, but I managed to make a pretty straight course for all that. The wind freshened and was quite cool. The sunlight, sparkling over the ocean, which now turned dark blue with a speck of white here and there to windward, warmed us enough to keep off actual chill, but the men who had taken off their coats to make a little more of a spread to the fair wind soon requested permission to put them on again. Sitting absolutely quiet as we were, the air was keener than if we were going about the sheltered decks of a ship.

On we went, the swell rolling under us and giving us a twisting motion. Sometimes we would be in a long hollow where the breeze would fail. Then, as we rose sternwrard, the little sail would fill, and away we would go, racing along the slanting crest of the long sea, the foam rushing from the boat's sides with a hopeful, hissing sound, until the swell would gain on us and go under, leaving the boat with her bow pointing up the receding slope and her headway almost gone, to drop into the following hollow and repeat the action.

The English sailor who had drank the water was now stone dead. Johnson gave me a look, and I began a conversation with Miss Sackett, endeavoring to engage her attention. A splash from forward made her look, and she saw what had happened. Then she turned and, looking up at me, placed her soft little hand on mine which lay upon the tiller.

"You are very good to me, Mr. Rolling, but I can stand suffering as well as a man," she said. "I thank you just the same." Then her eyes filled and she turned away her face. I found something to fix at the rudder head, and when I was through she was looking over the blue water where the lumpy trade clouds showed above the horizon's rim.

As the day wore on, the hunger of the men began to show itself. Jenks kept his wrinkled, leather face to the northward, looking steadily for a sail, but the other sailors glanced aft several times, and I noticed the strange glare of the eye which tells of the hungry animal. Some of these men had eaten nothing for twenty-four hours. One big, heavy-looking young sailor glanced back several times from the clew of his eye at the girl sitting aft. But I fixed my gaze upon him so steadily that he shifted his seat and looked forward.

Late in the afternoon some of the men insisted on eating the beef, and it was served to them. No ill effects followed, so all hands took their ration. This satisfied them for the time being, but I knew the thirst which must surely follow. I had been adrift in an open boat before in the Pacific. There had been sixteen men at the start, and at the end of four weeks of horror seven had been picked up to tell a tale which would make the blood curdle. The memory of this made me sick with fear and anxiety.

Johnson felt so much better from his meal that he stood in the bow with his little monkey-like figure braced against the mast, his legs on the gunwales. He said jokingly that he'd raise a sail before eight bells in the afternoon. Suddenly he cried out:—

"Sail dead ahead, sir!"

"'Tis no jokin' matter," growled Chips, angrily. "Shet yer head, ye monkey, afore I heave ye over th' side."

Johnson turned fiercely upon him.

"Jokin', you lummax! Slant yer eye forrads, an' don't sit there a-lookin' at yerself," he snarled.

"Steady, there!" I cried. "Where's the vessel?"

"Right ahead, sir, and standing down this ways, if I see straight."

I stood up on the stern locker and looked ahead. Sure enough, a white speck showed on the northern horizon, but I couldn't see enough of the craft's sails to tell which way she headed.

The men all wanted to stand at once, and it took some sharp talk to get them under control; but the young girl at my side showed no signs of excitement. I looked at her, and her gentle eyes looked straight into mine.

"I knew she would come," she said. "I've prayed all the morning."

In twenty minutes, spent anxiously watching her, the ship raised her topsails slowly above the line of blue, and then we saw she really was jammed on the wind and reaching along toward us rapidly.

"'Tis the *Pirit*, an' no mistake!" cried the carpenter. "Look at them r'yals! No one but th' bit av a mate, Trunnell, iver mastheaded a yard like that."

"The *Pirate*!" yelled Johnson, from forward.

And so, indeed, it really was.

I looked at her and then at the sweet face at my side. All the hard lines of suffering and fright had left it. The eyes now had the same gentle, trusting look of innocence I had seen the first morning we had taken off the *Sovereign's* crew. The reaction was too much for me. I was little more than a boy in years, so I reached for the girl's hand and kissed it.

When I looked up I caught the clew of Jenks' eye, but the rest were looking at the rapidly approaching ship.

XVIII

When the *Pirate* neared us, we could make out a man coming down the ratlines from the foretop, showing that she had evidently sighted us even before we had her. As she drew nearer still, we could see Trunnell standing on the weather side of the poop, holding to a backstay and gazing aloft at his canvas, evidently giving orders for the watch to bear a hand and lay aft to the braces. He would lay his mainyards aback and heave her to. Along the high topgallant rail could be seen faces, and on the quarter-deck Mrs. Sackett stood with our friend Thompson, better known in the Antipodes as Jackwell, the burglar. As I watched him standing there pointing to us, I thought of poor Jim.

"Wheel down," I heard Trunnell bawl as the ship came within fifty fathom. "Slack away that lee brace; steady your wheel."

Before the ship's headway had slackened we had out the oars and were rowing for her. In a moment a sailor had flung us a line, and we were towing along at the mizzen channels, with the men climbing aboard as fast as they could.

Miss Sackett was passed over the rail, and her mother took her below. I was the last one except Johnson to climb up. He stood at the bow ready to hitch on the tackles. But other men took his place, and as I went over the rail Thompson came and shook my hand warmly.

"Sink me, Mr. Rolling, but you've had a time of it, hey?" he said. "How are the men on the *Sovereign?* We've been standing along north and south for six days, expecting to pick you up, and here you are. It's all that Trunnell's doings. I was for going ahead the day we missed you, but that big-headed little rascal insisted on hunting for you after seeing you leave the wreck. Where's Jim and Phillippi, and the rest?"

The sincerity of his welcome had taken me off my guard, and I found myself standing there shaking his hand. Then I recovered myself.

"It's a pity Captain Thompson missed this ship the day she sailed," I said quietly. "We were informed the night before that he'd be with us. It might have saved the lives of some good men."

He let go my hand and smiled strangely at me, his hooked nose working, and his eyes taking that hard glint I knew so well.

"So you were really waiting for a man you'd never seen, hey? Was that the lay of it? And when I came aboard and said I was Thompson, you gulped down the bait, hey, you bleeding fool. Who the dickens do you think I am, anyhow?"

"I happen to know that you pass by the name of Jackwell," I said. "Here, Chips," I called, but the carpenter was already at my side. "What name did Jim give the captain, and what was his business?"

"'Tis no use av makin' any more av it, cap'n. We know all about ye. Th' best thing ye can do is to step down from the quarter-deck."

"Trunnell," said Thompson, with his drawl, "what d'ye think of these men coming back clean daft?"

The mate was close beside us, giving orders for the disposal of the small boat, and he turned and clasped my hand for the first time.

"Mighty glad t' see ye both back. I suppose the rest are aboard the *Sovereign*" said he, looking us over.

"And they come aboard with a tale that I'm some other man than Captain Thompson; that I knew that he was coming, and got aboard before him and went out in his place," said Jackwell. "Sink me, Trunnell, but I'm afeard you'll have to put them in irons."

"That's quare enough," said the mate, with a smile. "Come below, Rolling, and let's have yer yarn. You, too, Chips, ye'll need a nip of good stuff as well. I'm sorry ye've turned up with a screw loose. All right, cap'n. Square away when ye're ready. The boat's all right." And the little bushy-headed fellow turned and led the way down over the poop, entering the forward cabin, where the steward was waiting to tell us how glad he was we had turned up, and also serve out good grog with a meal of potatoes and canned fruit.

I was so tired and hungry from the exertions of the past twenty-four hours that I went below without further protest, Chips following sullenly.

"I'se sho nuff glad to see yo' folks agin, Marse Rolling," said the steward. "Take a little o' de stuff what warms an' inwigerates."

We fell to and ate heartily, and while we did so we told our story. Trunnell sat, and every now and again scratched his bushy head with excitement and interest while we told of the way Andrews had done. When we told how Jim had come to be aboard the *Pirate*, he walked fore and aft on the cabin deck, shaking his head from side to side, and muttering.

"Was Jim the only one who knew about the business?" he asked.

We told him he was, and that no one but Chips and myself had heard what the detective had said.

Trunnell sat with his hands in his hair for the remainder of the time we were filling ourselves. He said nothing further until Chips made some remark about his taking the ship in. Then he arose and stood before us.

"It may be as ye say, Rolling. I'd hate to doubt your word, and don't, in a way, so to speak. But discipline is discipline. You men know that. Our captain comes aboard with a letter sayin' as he's the Thompson what'll take the ship out. We has orders to that effect from the owners. It ain't possible another man could have known o' the thing so quick, and come aboard to take his place. Leastways, we hain't got no evidence but the word of a sailor who's dead, to the contrary. It may be as ye say, but we'll have to stick to this fellow until we take soundings. When we gets in, then ye may tell yer tale an' find men to back it. Don't say no more about it while we're out, for it won't do no good, an' may get ye both in irons. 'Twas a devil ye had for a shipmate when Andrews went with ye,—a terrible man, sure enough. I've insisted on standing backwards an' forrads along the track for nearly a week in hopes we'd pick ye up, an' I've nearly had trouble with the old man for waiting so long. He's heard o' the fracas, an' will stand along to pick up his third mate. I don't know as he'll care for Andrews, but he'll take the girl-mate sure if he's afloat."

"There's no use av makin' any bones av the matther, Mr. Trunnell," said Chips. "That third mate an' the murderin' devil ain't comin' aboard this here ship. Ef they do, I'll kill them meself whin they comes over th' side." And he arose, lugging out the revolver he had taken from the ruffian at the close of the fight.

I stepped into my room and brought forth my own, handing Chips some cartridges for his.

"I think the men will stand to us in the matter, Trunnell," I said.

The little mate looked sorrowfully at us both, and shook his great head slowly.

"'Tain't no use o' makin' a fuss," he said at last. "Discipline is discipline, an' you knows it. If the captain wants them fellows aboard, aboard they comes, and no one here kin stop them. There's only one captain to a ship. When his orders don't go, there's blood an' mutiny an' piracy an' death aboard. Put up your guns. Don't let's say no more about it till we raise them, for maybe they're gone under by this time. We won't reach the wreck anyways afore night."

It happened as he said. When we went on deck, the *Pirate* had swung her yards and was standing along in the direction we had come. Thompson, or rather Jackwell, walked fore and aft on the weather side of the poop, and gazed at each turn at the horizon ahead. A lookout was posted in the foretop, while the rest of the men lounged about the decks and discussed the situation and the tragedy of the day before.

Chips was for open mutiny, and Johnson backed him. All our men were in sympathy with us, and some were so outspoken that they could be counted on if a fresh fracas occurred. The majority, however, were so well under control that they appeared to be satisfied to obey orders under any conditions. The Englishmen were neutral. All except Jenks were silent or advised the recognition of the established authority, telling how we could square matters afterward with our enemies.

This shows how a sailor is at the mercy of any one who has been established in authority. If he resists in any manner, he is mutinous and is liable to the severest penalties. Here we were with every prospect of having Andrews and our third mate on board again, to go through some other horror, unless we turned pirates and took the ship. This was a risky thing to attempt, for if successful and there was any bloodshed, we would certainly either swing or pass under a heavy sentence. That is, of course, if we failed to prove that Thompson was the rascal Jim had told us he was. On the other hand, if we failed, there was the absolute certainty of being at the mercy of the rascal's cruelty, unless Trunnell would be able to control them all.

The little mate was a strange character. He believed in obeying orders under any conditions whatever, unless absolute proof could be had that the one who gave the orders was unauthorized to do so. In spite of his friendship for me, I knew full well that he would die rather than disobey the captain, no matter what the order was, provided he considered it a legitimate one. The fact that the men had committed horrible crimes did not in any manner disinherit them from the ship in his opinion. They should be dealt with afterward according to the law.

I took no part in an argument. Neither did Trunnell or the skipper. They both seemed satisfied of their position and took no pains to talk to the men as if they suspected a rising. I stood in the waist and remained looking steadily at the horizon until the sun dipped, and there was every prospect that night would come before we raised the black mast of the wreck. My pistol was in my pocket ready for instant use, and I saw by the bunch under Chips' coat that he was also ready. His small black mustache was worked into points under the pressure of his nervous fingers, and he sat on the hatch-combings apart from all save Johnson. The sailor walked athwartships before him on the deck as if to get the stiffness out of his little legs, which seemed now thinner than ever, as the setting sun shone between them through the curious gap.

The upper limb of the red sun was just touching the line of water when the man in the foretop hailed the deck.

"Wreck on weather bow, sir!" he bawled.

My heart gave a great jump and I looked at Chips. Johnson made a movement with his hand as if holding a knife and went to the weather rail and looked over.

"Weather maintopsail brace!" came the call from Trunnell. The men came tumbling aft and took their places.

"Lee braces, Mr. Rolling," he called again, and I crossed the deck, knowing that he would jam her as high as he could to make as far to windward as possible before darkness set in.

We braced her sharper, and she pointed a bit higher, but she could not quite head up to the black stick that showed above the horizon. The wind, however, was steady, and under her royals the *Pirate* was about the fastest and prettiest ship afloat. She heeled gently to the breeze and went through it to the tune of seven knots, rolling the heft of the long sea away from her clipper bows and tossing off the foam without a jar or tremble. I looked hard at the distant speck which was now just visible from the deck, and wondered how Andrews and his crew felt. I could see nothing of the *Sovereign's* hull, and hope rose within me. I found myself saying over and over again to myself, "She's gone under, she's gone under." Then just before it grew too dark to see any longer I went aft and took up the glass. Through it the black forecastle of the wreck showed above the sea.

XIX

It was quite dark before the *Pirate* had come up with the wreck. The skipper and Trunnell had gone below to their supper, and I had charge of the deck, with orders to heave the ship into the wind when we came abreast, and sing out for the mate to man the boat.

We were barely able to make within half a mile dead to leeward, but when we did, I backed the main yards and clewed up the courses, taking in the royals to keep from drifting off too fast in the gloom.

Trunnell came on deck and gave orders to get out the boat. She was soon at the channels, jumping and thrashing in the sea, for the breeze was now quite strong. The mate jumped into her with four men, and Thompson went to the break of the poop and told me I could go below to supper. Chips and the steward came aft, also, and we made out to eat a square meal in silence, each making a sign to his neighbor toward the back of his belt.

While we ate, listening for the sound of oars that would tell of the return of the boat, we could hear snatches of the sad talk of the two women in the after-cabin, through the bulkhead. This did not tend to raise our spirits, and we hurried through to be on deck when Trunnell returned.

Scarcely had we gained the main deck when we heard the regular sound of the oars and oar-locks. Soon the dim shadow of the boat was seen heading toward us, outlined against the light in the eastern sky where the moon was rising.

We took our places at the waist and awaited developments. Jackwell stood directly above me, and I could see his face with its glinting eyes turned toward me. His mustache was waxed into sharp points and curved upward, while his protruding chin and beak-like nose appeared to draw even nearer together. He was evidently quite well satisfied that he would be able to take care of his passengers, for he said nothing to me to indicate that he was disturbed by my proximity to the gangway.

I had decided to shoot Andrews the moment he came over the side, without a word. This much I had confided to Chips and Johnson. They would stand by me if there was a general attack, and we would make the best terms possible afterward.

The boat drew close aboard, and I could see the backs of the rowers swing fore and aft to the stroke. Then she shot alongside and was fast to the mizzen channels, and I stepped back ready for action. Jackwell noticed my move and drew his pistol. I drew mine, and glancing around I saw that the carpenter and Johnson were standing near, with their weapons at hand, and half a dozen sailors with them. I would not be alone.

A form sprang over the side, and I raised my weapon almost before I knew it. Then I recognized Trunnell.

"You can disarm that young fool, Trunnell," said Jackwell, putting away his gun. "It's lucky for him you've come back without any one, or I'd have shot him in half a second more."

The little mate came down the poop steps and went up to me.

"You better go below, Rolling," said he. "I didn't tell him," he added under his breath, "that you had said you'd mutiny afore I left, or he would probably have done for both you and Chips. He doesn't even know now that Chips was with you, so get into your room and pipe down."

I was so dazed at Trunnell coming back alone I could hardly talk. I looked again over the side to see if there was no mistake. All the men were now aboard, and only the empty craft was there, dancing at the end of her painter. Then I turned and followed the mate below, he stopping just long enough to give orders to hoist in the boat and swing the yards. Jackwell went to the wheel, and away the ship went to the westward, leaving the shadowy thing there on the eastern horizon to mark the end of a fine ship. I stopped a moment to look at the derelict, and the rising moon cast a long line of silver light across the sea.

Out in that shining track, a dark stick rose from the water. That was the last I saw of the *Sovereign*.

"Where were they?" I asked Trunnell, as we came into the cabin.

"Well," said the little mate, coolly, "since you've worked yourself up so much over the matter, and as we're a-goin' along on our course agin, as I suggested to the skipper afore we raised the wrack"—here he went to the pantry and brought out a bottle, and held it out to me.

"No," I said; "I don't want anything to drink. Tell me what became of the fellows on the wreck. It's my second watch, if I remember right, and I'll be ready to turn out at eight bells."

"Well," said Trunnell, "where they is an' where they is not, stumps me. Where a feller goes when he dies is mostly a matter o' guesswork, so I don't know as I can say eggzackly jest where them fellers is at."

Here he took a long drink, and wiped his mouth on the back of his hand. I put my gun in my room, and sat down at the cabin table, where he held the bottle as though undecided whether to take another drink or put it away in the pantry. Rum appeared to be easy of access on the ship, and I knew I could get it any time I wanted it.

"Well, ye see, the way of it ware like this," went on the mate. "I didn't take no stock o' those fellers bein' aboard a ship what had been afire, so when ye went into stays an' swore to do bloody murder an' suddin death to them fellers, I didn't let on to the old man. What's the use? says I. We ain't a-goin' to bring them back noways."

"Weren't they aboard?" I asked.

Trunnell gave me a long, keen look.

"Be ye tellin' o' this yarn, Rolling, or me?" he said.

I asked his pardon for interrupting.

"As I ware a-sayin' afore ye put in your oar, when I hears that ye both had told the truth o' the matter o' the fight, it appeared to me that them fellers couldn't be aboard that wrack. I told the old man so, but he ware fer standin' along after them anyways. Then I ware clean decided that the wrack had done fer them."

"Wasn't there a sign of them aboard?" I asked again.

"There's such a thing as bein' inquisitive," said Trunnell, looking at me with his keen little eyes from under their shaggy brows. "Them men ain't on that wrack—an' I told the skipper so, see?"

He pulled out his sheath-knife, went to the door of the cabin, and flung it clear of the ship's side. Then he came back.

"There's some such thing as justice on ships, when the fellers go too far; but discipline is discipline. The sooner ye get that through yer head, the better. As fer them men with Andrews, they had give up any right to live afore I got there. I told the old man that the chances were agin their bein' found there. I comes back and reports that they ain't there. That's all. Where they is I don't much keer. They is plenty o' sharrucks in this here ocean, and some parts o' them is most likely helpin' them. The rest is mostly in hell, I reckon, but as I says afore, that is a matter o' mostly guesswork."

A dim idea of the horror he had gone through came upon me.

"Good God, Trunnell," I said, "did you do it alone?"

"Well, there ware only one strong one in the lot—but look here, young man, if ye don't turn in pretty soon, ye'll be in trouble agin."

He poured himself out another drink, and put the bottle in the pantry. Then he went on deck, and I turned in to think over the spectacle that must have occurred aboard the blackened derelict. I could see Andrews's hope and the third mate's joy at being rescued. I could even picture them undergoing the wild joy I had just felt myself, when we had sighted the *Pirate*. Then came that nameless something. Had the men seen it? A rescuer coming aboard with a bloody knife in his belt, and the ship standing away again on her course for the States on the other side of the world!

There would be no explanations, and the blackened wreck, half sunken in the swell, would tell no tales. Trunnell was really a strange character.

"Discipline is discipline," I seemed to hear him saying all my watch below. His step sounded above my head as he walked fore and aft, during his watch; and during the periods of fitful slumber I enjoyed before eight bells struck, I fancied him a great giant whose feet struck with a thunderous sound at every stride. I was almost startled when his great bushy head was thrust into my room door, and he announced loudly that it was the mid-watch, and that I would need a stout jacket to ward off the cold.

XX

For the next three days we went along merrily to the northward, the beginning of the southeast trade behind us, and our skysails drawing full overhead. On the third day Cape Agullas was sighted on our beam. Then, away we went scudding across the South Atlantic Ocean for the equator.

Miss Sackett and her mother came on deck now and enjoyed the beautiful weather. The sufferings they had both gone through had made a deep impression upon them, and they were very quiet. The older woman would sit for hours in a faded dress saved from the wreck of the *Sovereign*, gazing sadly at the wake sparkling away in the sunshine astern. The bright gleams seemed to light up the memories of her past, and sometimes when I saw her she would have a tear trickling slowly down each cheek. Men as good as Sackett were scarce on deep water.

But the daughter was different. She was sad enough, at times. Being young, however, the loss of her father fell easier upon her. We often found time to chat together during the day watches on deck, and she showed a marked interest in the ship, and the people aboard, talking cheerfully of the future and the probable ending of the voyage. Jenks interested her and likewise Trunnell; but the sturdy mate paid little attention to her, devoting all his time to the affairs of her mother.

Thompson, or Tackwell, still commanded the ship, and Chips and I agreed there was no use in forcing matters with Trunnell against us. We would bide our time and wait for him on making harbor. He was doing well enough now, and since the women had come aboard he had been quieter in his cups, staying below when not sober enough to talk pleasantly. His mustache he curled with more care, and his dress was better than before, otherwise he walked the deck with the same commanding air, and drawled out his orders as usual. He was the most temperate at the very times when I expected him to go off into one of his ugly sarcastic fits, and was evidently trying to carry out the remainder of the voyage without any friction anywhere. This made matters easy for the mates.

During this period of good weather the routine duties of the ship took the place of the fierce excitement of the past. The bright sunshine cheered us greatly, and the spirits of all on board rose accordingly. The day watches were spent in healthy labor on the main deck, bending old sails and sending below the new ones. A ship, unlike a human being, always puts on her old and dirty clothes in fine weather, and bends her new and strong ones for facing foul.

The poultry and pigs, which nearly all deep-water ships carry, were turned loose to get exercise and air. The "doctor" worked up his plum-duff on the main hatch in full view of hungry men, and tobacco was in plenty for those who had money to pay for it, Trunnell giving fair measure to all who ran bills on the slop chest.

The little shaggy-headed fellow interested me more than ever now, and he was in evidence all day long. His hair and beard, which resembled the mane of a lion, could be seen at all times, from the poop to the topgallant forecastle, rising above the hatches or going down the gangways, where he attended to everything in person. Since the night when he came aboard with his bloody knife, I felt strangely toward him. He never alluded to the affair again in any way whatever, but went at his work in the same systematic and seaman-like manner that had, from the first, marked him as a thorough sailor. He was always considerate to the men under him, and many times when I expected an outburst of fierce anger, such as nine out of ten deep-water mates would indulge in at a stupid blunder of a lazy sailor, he simply gave the fellow a quiet talking to and impressed him with the absolute necessity of care in his work. We had plenty of men aboard, and the crew of the *Sovereign* were turned to each watch and made to do their share.

After a few days, Trunnell came to me and told me I might choose a third mate for him out of the men who had been in the *Sovereign's* crew. None of the men of the *Pirate* he said were up to a mate's berth, except Johnson, and he, poor fellow, couldn't read or write. Jenks was too slippery for me after his hand in the fracas, so I asked the steward to pick me out a man from forward, thinking he would be able to note the proper qualities better than myself, as he was thrown in closer contact with the men. The steward, Gunning, was a mulatto, as I have said, and he was of a sympathetic disposition. Among the men who had first come aboard from the wreck was an old fellow of nondescript appearance who had very thoughtfully seized several bottles of Captain Sackett's rum to have in the small boat in case of sickness. This was made possible by the flooding of the ship, which made it necessary for the men to live aft.

The old fellow had apparently enjoyed good health, and had saved a couple of bottles which he offered to the steward as a bribe for a recommendation. This kindness on the old man's part had appealed directly to Gunning, and he had sent him aft to me as the very man I wanted. He was very talkative and full of anecdotes, proving a most interesting specimen.

"I ain't been out o' sight o' land before in my life," said he, in a fit of confidence the first evening we divided watches, "but old Chris Kingle believed everything I told him, and here I am, third mate of this hooker, as sober as a judge, waitin' to get killed the first time I go aloft. Bleed me, but I'm in a fix; but it's no worse than I expected, for everything goes wrong nowadays."

"Well, what do you mean by coming aft here as mate when you know you can't fill the bill?" I roared, made furious at his confession.

"Cap," said he, as calmly as if I hadn't spoken, "some men is born great; some men tries to get great; and some men never has no show at all, nohow. Take your chances, says I. Mebbe I'm born great, an' it only needs a little opportunity to bring it out—like the measles. Anyways, I never let an opportunity fer greatness come along without laying fer it. I'm agin it now, an' if y' ever hear o' my bein' at sea agin, just let me know."

"If you ever see the beach again, you'll have reason to thank me, and I'll just tell you right now, you can make up your mind for double irons until we get to Philadelphia," I shouted.

"Bleed me, cap, that's just about what I didn't think you'd do," the lubber responded. "Give me a chance, 'n' if I'm no good as third mate, I'll probably do as fourth. Try me. If I'm born great, I'll show up. If I'm not, I can at least die great, or greater than I am. I've lived on land all my life, but I know something about sailing. I'm fifty-two year old come next fall, an' if I can't sail a ship after all I've seen o' them, I'll be willing to live in irons or brass, or enny thing."

"You go below and tell Mr. Gunning to come here to me," I said, in no pleasant tone, and as the fellow shuffled off to do as I said, his bloated, red features told plainly what it had cost him to overcome Gunning and get the steward into the state he must have been to recommend such a fellow for an officer aboard ship.

When Gunning came aft, he was so ashamed of himself that I let him go, and he picked a mate from one of the quartermasters of the watch, while I turned the old fellow to as a landsman. This had no effect on his loquacity, however, for he never lost an opportunity for telling a sad yarn full of the woes of this life and the anticipated ones in the world to come. He had drank much and thought little, except of his own sorrows and ill luck, but as his yearnings for sympathy did no harm, he was seldom repressed.

We were three months out before we struck into the rains to the southward of the line, so there was an accumulation of dirty clothes aboard that would have filled the heart of a laundress with joy—or horror.

The *Pirate* was running close on her water, for the port tank had sprung a leak, and there was no condenser aboard. The allowance had been set at two quarts per day for each man. This was barely enough to satisfy ordinary thirst and no more.

For the first day or two we made good headway into the squally belt. The heavy, black, and dangerous-looking clouds would come along about every half-hour, just fast enough to keep the men busy clewing down and hoisting the lighter canvas nearly all day long, for some would have a puff of wind ahead of them and some a puff behind, making it all guesswork as to how hard it would strike.

After the second day we had the doldrums fair enough, and there we lay with our courses clewed up and our t'gallantsails wearing out with the continuous slatting, as the ship rolled lazily on the long, easy equatorial sea. She was heading all around the compass, for there was not enough air to give her steering way; so, after dinner, all hands were allowed to turn out their outfits on the main deck for a grand wash. When we were under one of those squall-clouds, the water would fall so heavily that it would be ankle deep in the waist in spite of the half-dozen five-inch scuppers spouting full streams out at both sides. The waterfall was enough to take away the breath, standing in it, but all hands turned out stripped to the waist. The scuppers were plugged, and soon the waist of the ship, about forty feet wide and sixty long, looked like a miniature lake with the after-hatch rising like a snow-white island from the centre, and upon which a miniature surf broke as the water swashed and swirled with each roll of the ship. Here were hundreds of gallons of excellent water to wash in, and blankets, jumpers, flannels, etc., were soon floating at will, while the men seized whatever of their belongings they could lay hands on, and rubbed piece after piece with soap. The large pieces, such as blankets, were hauled into the shallows forward, where the ship's sheer made a gently sloping beach. Then they were smeared with soap and laid just awash, while the men would slide along them in their bare feet as though on ice, squeezing out great quantities of dirty suds. Afterwards they would be cast adrift in the deep water to rinse.

I came to the break of the poop and looked down upon the busy scene a few feet beneath on the main deck. The water here was fully two feet deep in the scuppers when the ship rolled to either side, and the men were almost washed off their feet with its rush. Some of them had climbed upon the island,—the main hatch,—where they sat and wrung the pieces of their apparel dry. Among these washers was my old third mate, now transformed into a somewhat shiftless sailor.

The old fellow's wardrobe was limited. It consisted of his natural covering in the way of skin and hair, one shirt, and a pair of badly worn dungaree trousers. The shirt he had worn during the entire cruise, and perhaps some time before, and as it fitted him tightly, and as his natural covering of hair on his chest was thick, it had gradually worked its way through the cloth, curling sharply on the outside, making the garment and himself as nearly one as possible. This had caused him no little inconvenience in washing, and it was with great difficulty he had removed the garment. He had spent half an hour rubbing it with a piece of salt-water soap, rinsed it thoroughly, and had it spread out on the hatch-combings. His work being finished, he sat near it, with his knees drawn up to his breast, his hands locked around his shins, and his face wearing an expression of deep and very sad thought.

Trunnell came out on the deck and had his things cast into the water with the rest. Then he peeled off his shirt and stood forth naked to the waist, a broad belt strapped tightly about him holding his trousers. His muscles now showed out for the first time, and I stood gazing at the enormous bunches on his back and shoulders. He was like some monstrous giant cut off at the waist and stuck upon a pair of absurdly short legs, which, however, were simply knots of muscle.

When he had finished his shirt, he turned over the rest of his belongings to Johnson to wash for him. Then his gaze fell upon the unhappy-looking old fellow on the hatch, who was holding his single shirt now in his hands, waiting for it to dry sufficiently for him to wear it again. As the rain fell in torrents every few minutes, this appeared an endless task, and the old man grew more sorrowful.

"There ain't nothin' in this world fer me," said he, sadly, cc not even a bloomin' shirt. Here I am shipwrecked and lost on a well-found ship, an' sink me, I ain't even able to change me clothes, one piece at a time."

"Ye'll soon be ashore agin, old feller," said Trunnell, "an' then ye'll have licker an' clothes in plenty."

"What's licker to me?" said the old man.

"Why, meat an' drink, when ye has to quit it off sudden like," said Trunnell.

"It's clothes I wants, not no rum. Can't ye see I'm nakid as Adam, except fer this old rag? I wouldn't mind if I ware signed on regular like the rest, 'cause I could take it out the slop chest in work. But here I is without no regular work, no chanst to draw on the old man, an' next month, most like, we'll be running up the latitoods inter frost. I'm in a hard fix, shipmate, an' you kin see it."

Trunnell seemed to be thinking for several minutes. Then he spoke.

"There's lots o' bugs an' things forrads, ain't there?" said he.

"If by lots ye means millions, I reckon ye're talkin'," said the man.

"Well," said Trunnell, "I'll tell ye what I'll do. You get a sail needle an' a line to it about half a fathom long, see?"

"I sees."

"Well, then ye go about between decks, an' in the alleyways, an' behind the bunks, an' around the galley, an' earn yer own outfit with that needle, see? When ye have a string o' bugs a-fillin' the string like clear up to the needle's eye, ye bring them aft to me, an' I gives ye credit fer them in clothes or grog, each string bein' worth a drink, an' a hundred worth a shirt or pants. Do ye get on to the game?"

"I get on to it well enough," said the fellow, "but what I wants to know is, whether ye'll take me whurd o' honner that I'll catch a string o' bugs afore night, an' give me the rum now to stave off the chill."

"I will," said Trunnell.

The old man rose from the hatchway, and struggled hard to get into his shirt. The garment had shrunk so, however, that the sleeves reached but to his elbows and the tails to his waist band. He seized the open front in his hand and looked solemnly at the mate with his sad eyes.

"Lead me to it! Lead me to it! For the Lord's sake, lead me to it!" he said quietly.

And Trunnell went into the forward cabin with the apparition following eagerly in his wake.

What a strange little giant he was, this mate! "Discipline is discipline," he would say, and no man got anything for nothing aboard his ship.

XXI

We crossed the line in 24 west longitude, running close to the St. Paul's Rocks. These strange peaks to the southward of the equator caused some interest aboard, rising as they do out of the middle of the ocean a mile or more in depth.

The air was hot and muggy the day we crossed into the northern hemisphere, and the light breeze died away again, leaving the ship with her courses clewed up, rolling and wallowing uneasily in the swell.

Jackwell, as I must always call him now, spruced himself up better than usual, and paid more attention to the ladies. He avoided me at every opportunity; but as neither Chips nor myself ever alluded to the story we had heard from Jim, his courage rose, and he became more familiar with the men.

Up to this time, we had not sighted a single sail since the *Sovereign*; but here on the line, where the fleets of the maritime world congregate to pick up the north or southeast trades, we sighted many ships bound both out and in.

One of these that happened near us was the *Shark*, whaling brig of three hundred tons, commanded by Captain Henry,—a man who had sailed in American ships engaged in the deep-water trade for years before he had taken to whaling. This vessel signalled us; and when we had answered and found out who our neighbor was, we were invited aboard.

Jackwell was willing to go with the ladies, as he thought it might prove a diversion. There was no chance for a breeze, and the ships were within half a mile of each other, with a smooth sea between. He insisted, however, that I go along to command the boat.

Chips and I had from the first decided to try and get a peep at the captain's trunk, and this might prove our chance. Gunning's tale of its great weight gave rise to many high thoughts; and if it were gold, much might be hoped for if we landed our man when we made port.

A few words with the carpenter was enough, and then I got the men at work hoisting out the boat. I found time to try and persuade Trunnell to take my place in the small craft, but he was firm. It would never do, he said, to leave the ship without a high officer aboard. "There's no telling, Rolling, just what might happen in this world while a feller is on the deep sea. No, sir; go ahead and enjoy yourself. There's a-goin' to be some line jokes, I reckon, aboard that brig. If the skipper ain't been acrost before, he'll be liable to catch the fun as well as the rest, but he don't know nothin' about sech things."

I was a little suspicious at Trunnell's determination to stay aboard, especially when I found out he knew the captain of the whaler very well. However, I had the small boat hoisted out and made ready for the passengers. This time there was a compass and water breaker aboard, and a foghorn in the stern sheets in case of need.

Mrs. Sackett was helped into the small craft, and her daughter followed, both women looking brighter than at any time during the cruise. Mrs. Sackett was not a bad-looking woman at any time, being of about the medium height, with a smooth complexion, and her figure finely proportioned. Her daughter seated herself beside her in the stern, and Jackwell climbed over the rail.

He was dressed in a very fine suit of clothes, his shirt-front white, and his waxed mustache curled fiercely. His glinting eyes had a somewhat humorous expression, I thought, and he appeared very well pleased with himself.

Trunnell came to the rail and leaned over. "Good luck to ye," he cried. "We'll expect ye back to dinner."

"Keep an eye on my room, and don't let the steward disturb the charts on my trunk until I come back. The last sight is worked out on the one lying on the table," replied Jackwell.

Then the oars fell across, and we shot out over the smooth ocean to the brig that rolled lazily half a mile distant.

The skipper appeared in a most humorous mood, which increased as did the distance between the ships.

He talked to Mrs. Sackett incessantly and actually had that lady laughing happily at his remarks. Miss Sackett did not rise to his humor, however, and her mother noticed it.

"Jennie, dear, why don't you laugh? Captain Thompson is so funny," she said.

"I will when he gets off a good joke, mother."

"Get off a good joke?" echoed the skipper. "Well, that's what I call hard. A good joke? Why, my dear child, I've gotten off the joke of my life to-day. Sink me, if I ain't played the best joke of the year, and on Trunnell too, at that. A good joke? ha, ha, hah!" and he threw his head back and laughed so loud and long that his mirth was infectious, and I even found myself smiling at him.

"Tell us what it is," said Miss Jennie.

"Oh, ho, ho, tell you what it is," laughed Jackwell, and his nose worked up and down so rapidly that I marvelled at it. His glinting eyes were almost closed and his face was red with exertion. "And suppose I'd tell you what it is, Miss Sackett? You wouldn't laugh. Not you. You couldn't rise to the occasion like your mamma. No, sink me, if I told you what it was, you wouldn't laugh; so you'll all have to wait till you get back aboard to hear it. But it's a good one, no fear."

We were now almost alongside of the brig, and could see her captain at the gangway, waiting to receive us. All along the rail strange faces peeped over at us.

"Way enough," cried Jackwell, and the oars were shipped. The boat swept alongside, and a ladder was lowered for us. I climbed out first to be able to assist the ladies, and as I gained the deck I was greeted by a strongly built, bearded man who looked at me keenly out of clear blue eyes.

"I'm glad to see you, sir," said he, holding out his hand.

I shook hands and turned to help Mrs. Sackett over the rail. Then came Miss Jennie, and last of all our captain.

Jackwell sprang up the ladder quickly, and stood in the gangway.

"How are you, sir, Captain Thomp—"

Captain Henry checked himself, looking at our skipper as though he had seen a ghost.

"Why, Jack—"

But Jackwell had put up his hand, smiling pleasantly.

"Jack it is, old man. You haven't forgotten the time I picked you up on the beach, have you?" he said, laughing. "Mrs. Sackett," he cried, turning, "allow me to introduce my friend, Captain Henry. Miss Sackett, also. Here's a skipper who hasn't forgotten the day I pulled him out of the water on the coast of South Wales, where he was wrecked. Sink me, but it's a blessing to see gratitude," he cried again, laughing heartily. "Fancy one skipper pulling another out of the sea, hey? Can you do that?"

"Well, I want to know," replied Henry. "I never knew you was a—"

"You never knew what, old man? What is it ye never knew? Sink me, it would fill every barrel you have below, hey? wouldn't it? What you never knew, nor never will know, would fill your little ship so full she'd sink, Henry, or I'm a soger. Ha, ha, hah! my boy; I don't mean to cast no insinuations at you, but that's a fact, ain't it? But what the dickens have you got going on aboard?"

He turned and gazed at the brig's main deck, where tubs of water and soapsuds were being poured into the trying-out kettles built in the brig's waist.

"Why," said Henry, "since you are a sea-capting, you must know the lay of it. Hain't you never crossed the line in a sailin' ship before?"

He had apparently recovered himself, and the surprise at meeting an old acquaintance appeared to give him pleasure.

Taking Mrs. Sackett by the hand, he led her aft up the poop steps, Jackwell following, keeping up a continual talk about whales and whaling skippers. Jennie and I followed behind and examined the brig's strange outfit.

The first mate, a man of middle age, lean and gaunt, came forward and introduced himself. He had sailed in every kind of ship, and was now whaling, he declared, for the last time. As I had made several "last voyages" myself, I knew that he meant simply to show involuntarily that he was a confirmed sailor of the most pronounced sort.

He showed us the lines and irons, the cutting-in outfit, and the kettles and furnace for boiling down the blubber. We followed him about, and I expressed my thanks when we arrived at the poop again, where he left us. Jennie was not interested, and the fact was not lost upon the old fellow, who turned away to join his mates at the kettles.

"Do you know, Mr. Rolling, I don't care a rap for ships," said she. "They don't interest me any more, and I don't think they are the place for women, anyhow."

"It would be mighty lonesome for some men if they acted on that idea and kept out of them," I answered.

We were all alone by the mizzen, the captains having gone below with Mrs. Sackett to show her the interior of the ship.

The young girl looked up, and I fancied there was just a sparkle of amusement in her eyes.

"Do you really think so?" she said. "Can't men find more useful occupations than following the sea,—that is, those who are lonely?"

"Some men are fitted to do certain things in this world and unfitted for others. It would be hard on those whose lines are laid out like that for them. You don't think a man follows the sea after his first voyage because he likes it, do you?" I said.

"Then for Heaven's sake why don't they stay ashore?" she demanded.

"Would you care for a man who would stay out of a thing that he was fitted for, simply because it was hard?" I asked her.

She blushed and turned away.

"I was not speaking of caring for any one, Mr. Rolling," she replied. And then she added quickly, "I think we will go below and see what they have for us."

"No, wait just one minute, Jennie," I said, taking her hand and stopping her gently without attracting the attention of the men forward. "This is the first time we've had a chance to talk of ourselves in two months. I want to ask you if you really meant that?"

"Meant what?" she said, stopping and turning around, facing me squarely.

"That you didn't care for any one?" I stammered, and I remember how my face burned.

She let me hold her hand and looked up into my eyes.

"I never said any such thing—that I didn't care for any one," she replied.

"Then do you, Jennie?"

She made no answer, and let her eyes fall. I let go her hand and drew myself up, for I was uncertain.

"I say, Rolling, what the deuce are you two doing?" bawled the voice of Jackwell from the companion, and then I realized that there was little privacy aboard a ship of three hundred tons.

We went aft guiltily, and met the rest coming up the companion with bottled beer and sandwiches which were served as refreshments. Chairs were set out by the old mate and two harpooners who had come aft, and the cook spruced himself up to get us out a plum-duff for lunch. From where we sat behind the poop rise, nothing could be seen forward, and here we ate and drank while Jackwell laughed and talked incessantly, being a completely changed man from the sarcastic and somewhat truculent skipper I had known for the last three months. It was finally suggested that as the awning was stretched, the plum-duff could be served on deck better than below in the stuffy cabin, so here we enjoyed the meal.

XXII

While we ate, Jackwell expanded more and more under the influence of duff and beer. He leaned back in his chair and gazed at the mainmast.

"What makes the top of your mast so black, hey? Is it the smoke from the kettles, or have you been afire? Sink me, Henry, there couldn't have been any such luck as your old hooker afire and being put out, hey? Ha, ha, hah! that would have been asking too much of the devil."

"It's hollow," said the old mate.

"What? Hollow? What the deuce is your mast hollow for?"

"Well, that is a question, isn't it, Mrs. Sackett?" said Henry. "Perhaps he asks you sometimes what a smoke-pipe is hollow for, don't he? I never seen such a funny man. But he'll never get over it, I want to know."

"Is it really hollow?" asked Jennie of the old mate.

"Yessum, it certainly is. Why, it's the smoke-pipe, you know," was the reply. "We have an engine in the lazarette that'll take us along more'n three knots in dead calm weather. It's been a lot o' help, when the wind has been light and ahead, fer picking up the boats. Ye know a whale always makes dead to windward, mostly, an' if the wind is light and we've got to go a long ways, the poor devils would most starve waitin' fer us, like they used to do in the old times. The lower mast is iron. There's lots of them that way now. The soot makes the canvas black sometimes, but there ain't no sparks to speak of ever comes out of that top, as it's mostly blubber we burns."

Jackwell became silent for several minutes, and then, as his eyes were still directed at the masthead, I looked again and noticed the topsail yard settled below the lower masthead.

"How do you suppose he keeps it up like that?" I asked Jackwell, trying to be civil.

"Keeps what up like what?" he said, in his old tone.

"The yard," I answered shortly.

"Oh, mostly by force of habit, I reckon," said he, nodding sarcastically at me and wrinkling his nose. "That's it, ain't it, Henry? Your yards stay mastheaded mostly by force o' habit, hey? They don't need no ropes."

I saw I was not forgotten, so afterward I kept quiet when he spoke. In a moment or two after this there was a wild yell from forward. This terminated into a deep bass roar, and we all jumped up to see what was the matter.

The form of a man sat on the starboard cat-head, and in his mouth was a horn of enormous size, the mouth being fully three feet across.

"Sooaye, Sooa-a-aye!" he roared. "Make way fer the great king o' the sea!"

I saw the fellow had on a long, rope-yarn beard and a wig to match, while a pair of black wings hung from his shoulders.

While he called, creatures swarmed over the bows. Men with beards and men without, some holding long spears and streamers, and some with three-pronged tridents, all having huge heads with grotesque faces, and forked tails which hung down behind.

"Hooray fer the king o' the sea!" bawled the fellow through the horn; and then the motley crowd yelled in chorus, some blowing huge conch-shells, and all making a most hideous racket.

Jennie stopped her ears and gazed, laughing at the throng. She had been across the line before in some of the older ships with her father, and knew of the practice. Mrs. Sackett and Captain Henry cheered and waved their handkerchiefs, but Jackwell sat silently looking on. Finally all of us went to the break of the poop, where we could get a better view, and just as we arrived, a monstrous form came over the knight-heads and stood forth on deck.

The fellow had a beard fully a fathom long, and he stood nearly two fathoms high, his feet being hoof-shaped. Gigantic black canvas wings hung from his shoulders, and a huge wig of rope-yarn, with the hair falling to his waist, sat on his head. He was escorted unsteadily to a seat upon the trying-out furnace.

"All who have to worship the king, come forth, an' stan' out!" yelled the man with the horn. This was greeted with cheers and blasts on the conch-shells.

Some of our men had never been over before, and one of the boat's crew confessed. He was quickly seized and brought before King Neptune.

"Sit ye down, right there in that there cheer," said the king, scowling fiercely.

The fellow sat down and stared, smiling at the monster.

"Have ye paid fer comin' acrost this here latitood, me son?" asked the king.

"No," said the sailor.

"No, what?" roared the king.

The chair was placed on the edge of the main kettle and the monster simply raised his hand to one of his retainers. This fellow tilted it up, sailor and all, into the smother of suds and water. Instantly there were roars of laughter, as all hands watched the man trying to get clear of the slippery iron tank. Every time he would get a hold, his fingers would be rapped sharply, and down he would go, floundering about. He was finally let off with a fine of a plug of tobacco, all his belongings save the clothes he had with him.

Other men followed, for the whaler had a crew of thirty-five. Some were shaved with a barrel hoop for a razor, and tar for lather, being finally released for some tobacco.

"Come aft, O king," bawled Henry, after the fun had grown fast and furious. "Come aft, and get a donation from the ladies."

The great fellow was escorted unsteadily to the poop, where he saluted the women.

"Have ye never paid toll to go to the other world, yet?" asked the king.

"No," said Jackwell, who was getting tired of the fun, "I ain't never been acrost, and I ain't a-going to pay toll."

"Shall he pay?" asked the king of Henry.

"Sure," was Henry's response.

Instantly the giant sprang upon the deck, getting clear of his stilts by some means or other. He seized Jackwell tightly around the body, and rushing to the rail, sprang into the sea, his followers yelling themselves hoarse with delight.

When they were hauled aboard, Jackwell was in a fury. I expected him to shoot the sailor who had the audacity to pitch him overboard, but he controlled himself. The incident, however, ended the fun aboard the brig, Henry, between fits of laughing, telling the mate to serve all hands with all the grog they wanted.

"Do not wait for me, madam," said Jackwell, to Mrs. Sackett. "I shall not come aboard my ship in this condition. You get Mr. Rolling to take you and your daughter, and I'll follow, after Captain Henry has given me a new suit of clothes."

This appeared to be the best thing to do, as the brig's men were now getting boisterous with the grog, and our men were drinking also. The ladies were tired of the performance, although they had enjoyed some of it very much, and they were glad when I called away the boat's crew to take them back to the *Pirate*.

Jackwell appeared at the rail as we started off.

"Rolling," said he, "tell Trunnell not to stay awake at night worrying about my health. This bath will not strike in and tickle me to death as you might be agreeable enough to suppose."

"Hurry and change your clothes, captain," cried Mrs. Sackett.

"Madam," said he, with great solemnity as the oars were dropped across, "do not grieve for me. It will make me unhappy for the rest of my pious existence if you do. Fare thee well."

We were now on our way back to the ship, and he stood a moment, waved his hand, and then disappeared down the companionway.

In ten minutes we were aboard again, and I met Chips in the waist as I stopped to get a piece of tobacco.

"Well, what was it?" I asked.

"Faith, an' I got caught," said Chips, with a sickly grin.

"How was it?" I asked. "Come, tell me, while Ford and Tom get the cushions out of the boat;" and I drew the carpenter into the door of the forward cabin where Trunnell couldn't see us.

"'Twas a fine thing ye made me do, but no matter," he began. "Ye see, whin ye had started well on yer way to th' fisher, I thinks now is th' time av me life. Trunnell ware sitting and smokin' on the wheel-gratin', an' all ware as quiet as ye please. I wint below whistling to set him off his guard, like; an' whin I sees me way clear I takes me chance at the after-cabin, an' in I goes. I stopped whistlin' whin I makes th' enthry, an' I steered straight fer th' chist forninst the captin's room. The door ware open, an' I see the chist ware a little trunk av a thing, no bigger than a hand-bag, so to speak. Up on top av it ware a pile av charts an' things sech as th' raskil sung out to Trunnell not to touch. 'Twas a cute little thing to do; fer how I could get inter th' outfit without a-movin' them struck me.

"I finally grabs th' side av th' trunk an' tries to lift it. Ye may say I lie, but s'help me, I cud no more lift that little trunk than th' ship herself.

"Gold? Why, how cud it 'a' been anything but solid gold? I cud lift that much lead easy. I stopped a minit and took out me knife, me mind made up to thry th' lock. I give wan good pick at ut, an' thin I hears a sort av grunt. There ware Trunnell a-lookin' right down at me from th' top av th' after-companion.

"Sez he, 'An' what may ye be a-doin' wid th' old man's trunk,' sez he.

"'Sure 'tis me own I thought it ware, by th' weight av it,' sez I.

"'Is it so heavy, thin?' sez he.

"'Faith, ye thry an' lift it,' sez I.

"He come down th' ladder an' took a-hold, shutting th' door to keep th' steward from a-lookin' in. Thin he takes hold av th' thing an' lifts fer th' good av his soul. Nary a inch does it move.

"'I wud have opened it, but I heard th' captin's order not to disturb th' charts atop av it,' sez I.

"'Ye would, ye thafe,' sez he. 'An' if ye had, inter irons would ye go fer th' raskil ye are. I never thought ye ware so bad, Chips,' sez he.

"''Tis a victim av discipline I am, fer sure, thin,' sez I. 'Ye know I wud no more steal th' matther av a trunk than fly.'

"'An' who give ye th' order, ye disciplinarian?' sez he.

"'Me conscience,' sez I.

"'Ye better go forrads an' tell yer conscience th' fact that it's a bad wan fer an honest man to travel wid,' sez he. 'An' tell him also to mind what I says about obeyin' orders aboard this here ship. If yer conscience iver wants to command a ship, he don't want to forget that discipline is discipline, an' whin it comes to thavery, discipline will get ye both in irons. Slant away afore I loses my temper an' sails inter ye,' sez he.

"So here I am, all in a mess wid that little mate. But th' trunk av gold is safe on th' cabin floor."

I had nothing to say further than that the matter couldn't be helped. If the trunk was all right, we might land a fortune yet in the reward Jim had told us about. Jackwell must have made off with a snug little sum. I climbed over the side again with some of the skipper's clothes, and we started slowly back to the brig to get him.

Ford was rowing bow oar, and Johnson aft, and both rowing easily made us go very slow. However, there was no hurry. Jackwell would in all probability take several drinks after his bath, and we would only have to wait aboard the whaler for him until he was ready. The sea was so smooth that the boat hardly rippled through it, and the sun was warm, making me somewhat drowsy. The two men rowed in silence for some time, and then Ford suddenly looked ahead to see how we were going.

"What's the matter with the bloomin' brig?" said he, rowing with his chin on his shoulder.

I looked around, and it seemed as though we had already gone the full distance to her, and yet had as far again to go. The *Pirate* was certainly half a mile away and there was the brig still far ahead.

"Give way, bullies," I said. "Break an oar or two."

The men made a response to the order, and the boat went along livelier. I looked at the brig, and suddenly I noticed a thin trail of smoke coming from her maintop where the opening in the lower masthead should be.

We were now within fifty fathoms of her, when Jackwell came to the rail aft and looked at us.

"Give way, bullies, you're going to sleep." I said.

In a few moments we were close aboard, but as we came up, the brig slewed her stern toward us, and then I noticed for the first time that she was moving slowly through the water. There was no wind, and I knew in a moment that she was under steam. She drifted away faster, and the men had all they could do to keep up. Jackwell leaned over the taffrail and gazed calmly down at us.

"That's it, boys, give it to her. You'll soon catch us and be towing us back again. Sink me, Rolling, but you're the biggest fool I ever saw," he said.

I saw the water rippling away from the brig's side, and now could see the disturbance under her stern where a small wheel turned rapidly.

"Throw us a line," I cried to Jackwell.

"What d'ye want a line fer? Are ye a-going with us to the Pacific, or are ye jest naturally short of lines, hey?"

"Throw us a line or we'll have to quit," I cried; "the men can't keep up as it is."

Jackwell let down the end of the spanker sheet, and Ford grabbed it, taking a turn around the thwart. The boat still rushed rapidly along.

"Rolling," said the captain of the *Pirate*, "hadn't you better go home and tell Trunnell he wants you? Seems to me you'll have a long row back in the hot sun. I'd ask you all aboard, but this ship ain't mine. She belongs to a friend who owes me a little due, see? Now be a sensible little fellow. Rolling, and go back nicely, or I'll have to do some target practice, or else cut this rope. Give my kindest regards to the ladies, especially Mrs. Sackett. Tell her that I wouldn't have dreamed of deserting her under any other circumstances, but this brig has got the devil in her and is running away with me. I can't stop her, and I can't say I would if I could. That infernal King Neptune has got hold of her keel and is pulling us along. Good-by, Rolling; don't by any possible means disturb the charts on my trunk. There, let go, you Ford."

Ford cast the line adrift, and the boat's headway slacked. The brig drifted slowly ahead, going at least three knots through the smooth water. A long row of smiling faces showed over the rail as we came from under her stern. One fellow, waving his hand, cried out to report Bill Jones of Nantucket as "bein' tolerable well, thank ye." It was evident they knew nothing of Jackwell and treated the going of the brig as a good joke on greenhorns.

"That beats me," said Ford, panting from his last exertions.

"An' me too," said Johnson. "If we'd had Tom and one or two more along we'd have beat her easy. But ain't he a-comin' back at all at all?"

"I hardly think we'll see Captain Thompson any more this voyage," I answered savagely; "but by the Lord Harry, he's left his trunk all right."

XXIII

When we rowed back to the ship, Trunnell was looking at us through the glass up to the time we came under the *Pirate's* counter. He evidently could see that our skipper wasn't with us, and it seemed as if he could not quite make up his mind to the fact, but must keep looking through the telescope as though the powerful glass would bring the missing one into view. We ran up to the channels, and he looked over the side. A line of heads in the waist told of the curiosity among the men forward.

I said nothing, and nothing was said until the painter was made fast and Ford had sprung on deck.

"He ain't with ye, Rolling?" asked Trunnell.

I was too much disgusted to answer. The empty boat was enough to satisfy any reasonable person.

Chips came to the rail and leaned over as I came up the chain-plates. "'Twas so, then? Th' raskil! But what makes th' bloody hooker move? She's slantin' away as if th' devil himself ware holdin' av her fore foot!"

"Steam, you poor idiots," I cried out, in disgust, for it was evident that even Trunnell couldn't tell what made the *Shark* get headway, although now the smoke poured handsomely from her masthead.

Trunnell scratched his bushy head and seemed to be thinking deeply. Then he put down the glasses and led the way aft without a word, Chips and I following. We went below and found Mrs. Sackett and Jennie in the saloon.

"Where's the captain?" they asked in a breath.

"Faith, an' he's changed ships, if ye please," said Chips.

"And left a little thing behind he would have liked to have taken with him," I said.

"What was the matter?" they both asked.

Chips and I tried to tell, but we soon made a tangle of it, the only thing coherent being the fact that the fellow was a crook and had left his trunk behind. This was so heavy that Chips had failed to lift it.

"I always knew he was not a sea-captain," cried Jennie. "I don't see how you men let him fool you so badly."

Chips and I looked at the mate, but he simply scratched his head.

"Discipline is discipline," he said. "He ware capting o' this here ship, an' there ware no way to do but obey his orders. No, sir, discipline is discipline, an' the sooner ye get it through your heads, the better."

"But he isn't captain any longer," I said.

"Well, I don't know about that," said Trunnell. "If he ain't a-comin' back, he ain't capting, sure. But ye can't tell nothin' about it. He may come aboard agin in a little while an' want to know why we didn't wait dinner for him."

"He sho' would take his trunk," said Gunning, "an' dat's a fact."

"Why would he?" asked Mrs. Sackett.

"'Cause he take good care o' dat trunk, ma'm. He sleep wid one eye on it an' his gun handy. I come near gettin' killed onct when I come into de cabin, suddin' like, while he was at work ober de things inside."

"For Heaven's sake, let's look at it," said Mrs. Sackett.

"'Tis th' best thing we cud do," said Chips. "'Tis no less than solid gold he stowed in it. Faith, it's as heavy as th' main yard."

Mrs. Sackett led the way to the captain's room, and Trunnell made no farther resistance. She opened the door, and we crowded inside. There lay the trunk on the floor or deck ahead of us.

"Try yer hand at th' liftin' av th' thing," said Chips to me.

I reached down and took hold of the handle at the side. Pulling heavily, I lifted with all my power. The trunk remained stationary.

"Dere's nothin' but gold in dat thing, sho'," said Gunning.

"Well, for Heaven's sake! why don't some one open it?" cried Jennie.

"An' have him a-comin' back aboard, a-wantin' to know who had been at it, hey?" said Trunnell. "I didn't think ye ware that kind o' missy."

"Nonsense!" I said. "He isn't coming back. Even if he is, it won't hurt to lift it, will it?"

"No, I don't know as it will, only it might upset them charts," said Trunnell.

"Try it," I said. "See if it's gold. It'll clink when you shake it, sure."

The little giant stooped and gave a grunt of disdain. "I reckon there ain't nothin' that size I can't lift," said he, in a superior tone, which was not lost on the women. Trunnell seldom bragged, and we crowded around, looking for quick results.

"A little bit o' trunk a-breakin' the backs o' a pair o' fellows as has the impudence to say they are men an' question the discipline o' the ship!" he said, with a loud grunt of disgust. "Stan' clear an' let a man have a chanst. If it's gold, an' ye're right, it'll rattle an' jingle fast enough; an' I hopes then ye'll be satisfied."

He took a strong hold of the leather handle at the side and braced his little legs wide apart. It was evident he would put forth some power. Then he set the great muscles of his broad back slowly, like a dray horse testing the load before putting forth his strength. Slowly and surely the little mate's back raised. He grew red in the face, and we peered over the treasure, hoping it would rise and give forth the welcome jingle.

Suddenly there was a ripping sound. Trunnell straightened up quickly, staggered for an instant, and then pitched forward over the trunk, uttering a fierce oath.

Mrs. Sackett screamed. Jennie burst into a wild fit of laughter. Chips and Gunning stood staring with open mouths and eyes, while Trunnell picked himself up, with the trunk handle in his iron fist.

"Faith, an' ye are a good strong man," said the carpenter. "Ye'd make a fortune as a porter a-liftin' trunks at a hotel."

"He can lift a little thing like that," said Jennie, mimicking the mate's tone to perfection.

Trunnell was now thoroughly mad. If the trunk contained gold, he would soon find out.

"Bring yer tools, an' don't stan' laffin' like a loon, ye bloody Irishman," he said to Chips, and the carpenter disappeared quickly. He returned in a moment with a brace and bit, a cold chisel, and a hammer.

"Knock off the top," said Trunnell.

"Discipline is discipline," whispered Jennie; "and I don't want to be around if the captain comes back."

Trunnell was too angry to pay attention to this remark, so he looked sourly on while the carpenter cut off the rivets holding the lock.

"There ye are," he said, and we crowded around to look in while the mate raised the lid.

Off it came easily enough. We stood perfectly silent for an instant. Then all except Trunnell burst out laughing. The trunk was empty!

"Well, sink me down deep, but that ware the heaviest air I ever see," said Trunnell. Then he picked up a slip of paper in the bottom and looked at it a moment. It had writing on it, and he unfolded it to read. I looked over his shoulder and read aloud:—

"MY DEAR LITTLE MATE: When you get this here billee ducks, don't do anything rash. Remember the discipline of the ship, first of all, and then take the dollar bill here and get somebody to cut your hair fer ye, as it's too loing fer a man of sense and is disagreeable to the ladies. If ye thought ye had a pot of gold in this here outfit, ye get left, sure, and no mistake. Remember money's the root of all evil and thank yer Lord ye ain't got none. There ain't no answer to this note; but if ye feel like writing at enny time, address it to Bill Jackwell, care of anybody at all what happens to be around at the time I'm there—see? Some day we'll meet agin, fer I'm stuck on the sea and am going to buy a boat and appoint ye as captain, only yer must cut yer hair and trim up yer beard some. That's all."

Trunnell held the dollar bill he had unfurled from the note in his hand and dropped the note back into the trunk.

"'Tis screwed fast wid nine big bolts to th' deck," said Chips, who had examined the outfit carefully.

Trunnell scratched his bushy head thoughtfully for a moment longer. "Is there any sech thing as a few men aboard this ship?" he asked.

I said I thought there was.

"Then man the boat and row, for the love o' God!" he roared, springing up the companionway to the deck, leaving us to follow after him.

XXIV

When we reached the deck and looked after the brig, we found that we had spent more time below than at first imagined. The *Shark* was hull down to the southward and evidently going along steadily at a three-knot rate. The sun was almost on the horizon, and if we started after her, the chances were that night would fall long before we could lessen the distance between us materially. Sober appreciation of the affair took the place of Trunnell's impetuosity.

"We'll niver see him agin," said Chips, hauling heavily on the boat tackles.

"There's no use, Trunnell," I cried; "we can't catch that brig in a whale-boat."

He was already hesitating, and stood scratching his shaggy beard.

"Avast heavin' on that tackle," he bawled. Then he turned to me. "You're right, Rolling, we've lost a fortune an' the rascal too, but it ain't no use making bigger fools of ourselves. Stow the boat. After that send Johnson aft to me with a pair o' scissors. You an' Tom can set the watches, fer ye see I'm capting of her now. Ye might say, on the side like, that the first burgoo eater what comes along the weather side o' the poop while I'm on deck will go over the rail. There's a-goin' to be some discipline aboard the hooker, or I'll—well, there ain't no tellin' just what I won't do. I'm capting o' this here ship, an' ye might jest as well muster the men aft to hear the news."

Then he disappeared down the companion aft, and I sent Johnson to him with the shears as he had ordered.

When Trunnell came on deck again in the evening, his beard was a sight to be remembered. It looked as though a rat had nibbled it in spots. His hair was equally well done by the artist, but Jackwell's last order had been obeyed. The men were mustered aft, and Trunnell announced that he was the man they wanted to stand from under. They remained silent until Johnson suggested that three cheers be given for the new skipper. Then all hands bawled themselves hoarse. That was all. I was now the first mate and took my meals at the cabin table, where Jennie and her mother had been wondering at Trunnell's dexterity with his knife. The little mate appeared to realize that a certain amount of dignity and dress were necessary for the maintenance of correct discipline aboard, and he accordingly changed his shirt once a week and wore a new coat of blue pilot cloth. He sat at the head of the table, and went through his knife-juggling each meal, to the never ending amusement of Jennie, and admiration of Gunning, who swore that, "dey ain't no man afloat cud do dat no better." He, however, came through the rest of the cruise without even cutting his lip.

My duties and rating being those of a first mate, I had no longer the pleasure of being intimate with Chips and the rest forward. The carpenter, steward, and "doctor" had the quartermaster, Tom, from Trunnell's watch for a second mate and companion at the second table. Tom was a Yankee and a good companion, so the change was satisfactory all around. I sometimes looked in at the carpenter's room in the forward house, where he and a few chosen spirits would be holding forth upon some nautical subject, but I had to cut my visits short, for they worried Trunnell. Being suddenly raised did not quite inspire the necessary respect in his eyes, unless the person promoted showed unmistakable dignity and authority by dressing down all who came in contact with him. For some time it was pretty hard to speak to our little skipper. He disliked anything he imagined might tend to lessen the discipline aboard and had a horror of a mate or captain being familiar with the men.

My room was still in the forward cabin, but I now spent much time in the saloon, and helped Trunnell to shift his belongings aft to Jackwell's cabin. The truculent knave had left little behind him save a lot of old clothes, bonds which were not negotiable, and some wrappers used by the bank of Melbourne for doing up packets of bills. Upon one of these was a mark of fifty pounds sterling, showing that Jackwell's assets, unless enormous, could be made to fit in a very small space. He probably carried all he owned upon his person.

We went through everything in the cabin carefully, but the only thing of interest discovered was the photograph of a plump young woman torn fairly in two, the lower half bearing the inscription in Jackwell's handwriting, "Good riddance to bad rubbish."

I had found this in the chart case and had examined it some minutes without comment, when Miss Sackett took it from me. She gazed at it a moment, and cried out, "Why! it's the third mate."

I instantly seized it again and looked carefully at the features, and then it was plain enough. There he was, in a neat fitting bodice, the curly blond hair stylishly dressed, and the plump cheeks showing just the faintest trace of the dimples of our former third officer. I looked at the back of the photograph. It had the name of a Melbourne artist upon it, and beneath, in a female hand, the written words, "Yours lovingly, Belle."

Trunnell heard Jennie's exclamation and came up. He took the picture from me and gazed long at the face. Then he gave a sigh which sounded like a blackfish drawing in air, handed it back to me, and went up the companionway, scratching his head in the manner he did when much disturbed. He said not a word, nor did he mention Mr. Bell's name, and that night at supper he never raised his eyes from his plate. Afterward in the mid-watch he came on the poop and walked fore and aft for three long hours without so much as speaking to me or asking the man at the wheel the vessel's course. He finally went below, carrying the odor of grog along with him. He came on deck many nights after this and walked fore and aft in silence, as though brooding over some unpleasant subject, and we were clear of the trade and knocking about in the uncertain latitudes before he appeared to be anything like himself again.

I avoided any subject relating to the earlier part of the voyage and tried to cheer him. I thought he had suffered keenly, and was glad when he stopped drinking and looked me in the eyes without letting his gaze fall in confusion. Sometimes I caught myself wondering at the reticence of the men who had rowed him to the burnt wreck that night, but I found that no one had boarded her except Trunnell and he had sent the boat astern.

Tom, the quartermaster, made mate under me, was a good sailor. He did his work thoroughly, and everything went along without friction throughout the rest of the voyage to the Breakwater. We picked up the northeast trade in a few days, and hauled our starboard tacks aboard, bracing the yards sharp up until it gradually swung more and more to the eastward, letting us off on a taut bowline for the latitude of the States.

The *Pirate* showed herself to be the fast ship she had always been, for we made the run up the trade in less than three weeks. Trunnell took such pride in her that all hands were tired out before we ran over the thirtieth parallel, with the scrubbing, painting, holy-stoning, etc., that he considered necessary to have her undergo before arriving in port. As mate of the ship, I had much opportunity to command the deck alone; that is, without the supervision of any one. Of course, I can't say I spent much time alone on deck, even when in charge; but I would never let social matters interfere with work sufficiently to merit a rebuke from the little skipper. He soon manifested a disposition to be alone during his watch on deck, and at first I believed this to be due to the exalted dignity of his position. It hurt me to think he should be so changed, and I pondered at the peculiarities of mankind for many days. After awhile, however, he became absorbed in a game of checkers with Mrs. Sackett which lasted two weeks. Then I forgave him. Whenever he saw Jennie and myself on deck, he would make haste to get through his business there, and dive below again. This kindly interest on his part was kept up until we raised the Delaware Capes.

How good the land smelled, and how distinctly. It seemed incredible that one could smell the land twenty miles away, almost before the color of the water began to change. Yet it was strong in the nostrils; and even one of the pigs we had not eaten, but had brought back alive, squealed incessantly, as though instinctively feeling that the voyage was over.

It was late in the afternoon, but the men were mustered aft, in the time-worn way of merchant-men, to sign off. Nearly all had bills on the slop-chest for tobacco or clothes. As each went over the poop he gazed at the line on the western horizon and smiled gladly. It meant a new life for more than one. Among the last to go was the old landsman whom Trunnell had given a chance to earn his clothes by bug-hunting. He smiled sadly at the setting sun over the dark line which meant home. Then he shook out several strings of vermin, and holding them at arm's length, stopped at the cabin window. His cheap trousers failed to reach the tops of his coarse shoes, and the gap showed the skin on meagre ankles. I was interested to know what he would take.

"What d'ye want?" asked Trunnell.

"I come for a yaller silk ban'kercheef," said he, offering the strings.

"Don't yer think ye'd better get some o' them woollens? It'll be cold on the beach."

"I got clothes a plenty. I want a yaller silk ban'kercheef. Yer got one, for Sam tole me so. I'm a-goin' ashore to Hennery's, an' I ain't goin' like no clown without a wipe. Kin I have it?"

The handkerchief was passed out, and the old fellow went forward smiling.

What a strange thing is the end of a deep-water voyage! Men who have been living together for months through suffering and hardship will go over the ship's side with a cheery farewell. They may meet for a few moments at the office to draw their pay, and then take a drink all around. That is all. They seldom see or hear of each other again. The world goes on, and they drift about, taking what part in affairs Fate has in store for them. One should come back aboard the ship the day after she makes her dock and look into the deserted forecastle and about the lonely decks, where so much has taken place, to realize man's lonely mission. The old ship-keeper, sitting alone smoking on the hatchway in the evening before unloading begins, will affront one with his presence. Where are the men, rough, honest, coarse, or even bad, that used to sit there so often in the twilight of the dog-watch? There is a strange yearning to see them again. I watched the sun go down with a feeling of mingled joy and sorrow,—joy for the return to the States, and sorrow for the parting which must soon take place between my shipmates.

When we came to an anchor and made ready to go ashore, the little giant Trunnell came up to say good-by to the ladies. I had decided to accompany them to the city.

When he shook hands, the tears ran down out of his little eyes and trickled over his bushy beard to the deck.

"I wishes ye all the best o' luck," said he, and he fumbled in his pocket for a moment, letting a small piece of paper escape and flutter to the deck. I stooped and picked it up, glancing at the writing on it. The words were:—

Mrs. William Sackett, 25 Prince St., E.C., London, Eng.

He snatched it from me and seized my hand, gripping it so hard I almost cried out.

"Go along, ye lucky dog," he cried. "Say good-by to Chips an' the rest afore ye goes ashore. We'll be berthed an' paid off when ye comes back."

I said good-by to the men at the gangway, and then helped the ladies over the side into the boat, seating myself in the stern-sheets between them.

"I should think you'd be thankful to get in at last," said Jennie.

"Yes," I whispered; "but I have no objections to sailing again as a mate."

Her hand closed upon mine behind the backboard.

"Neither have I," she breathed in return.

"Whose mate?" I asked her.

But that's an old story.